ZHIRUTO

TAMSIN LEY

TWIN LEAF PRESS

Paperback version
ISBN-13: 9781950027439
Copyright © 2021 Twin Leaf Press

$\mathcal{L}$ora poured two glasses of champagne and offered one to the blue-skinned man sitting across from her at the table. Stars glittered overhead, and a few couples were dancing in front of the stage where a live band played. She had to give Georgie credit—the alien charity auction had so far been a success, raising more money for the animal shelter than all the previous fundraisers combined. She also had to admit that her worry about being set up on a date with a big-eyed, six-tentacled alien from Area 51 had been unfounded.

Every alien at the auction was positively scrumptious—if they even were aliens. She still had her doubts, though their blue skin looked amazingly realistic.

Extraterrestrials had supposedly landed in Beijing several decades ago. They'd showed off for the cameras, talked to a few dignitaries, then disappeared without a trace. Most people believed the visit had been a hoax, but Lora's friend Georgie insisted this Intergalactic Dating Agency thing was legit. Then again, Georgie's mom used to tell stories about being abducted. *Whatever.* Lora was willing to go along with the cosplay to make money for the shelter.

Her date wore a navy blue suit and looked like a broad-shouldered member of the Blue Man Group, bald head and all. However, his stoic silence was giving her a bit of a creepy vibe.

"So, have you been to Earth before?" she asked, trying to initiate alien small talk. She pushed one of the champagne flutes toward him, wrapping Pepper's leash tighter around her free hand. She regretted bringing the gangly Redbone Coonhound along—the guy couldn't seem to take his attention off the dog.

Her date turned his gaze to her, his eyes a solid black that was hard to get used to. "No."

A piercing scream erupted at a table behind her.

At almost the same moment, her date's body seemed to quiver. Not like someone with a chill or even a person with palsy—he actually *quivered,* like his body was made of Jell-o. Then he collapsed inward, reduced to a glob of glistening blue slime in the seat of his chair.

Lora gaped, then stood to pull the hem of her crimson ball gown out of the way of the gelatinous sludge rolling off the seat toward her. *Oh, hell no.* Georgie had promised there would be no slime.

Her date—or what was left of him—landed on the grass with a plop.

More screams were coming from other tables, and she glanced around, heart pounding fast and hard. Everywhere she turned, blue-skinned aliens were dissolving. A white poodle darted past, dragging its leash. A woman ran after it shouting, "They must have death rays!"

Most of the alien guests had looked like blue humans, but the two gray aliens with horns and wings now perched on the stage several yards away. Now one of them flew upward—actually flew!—and batted something from the sky.

Lora gaped, all doubt about these being real aliens dispelled.

A drone smashed to the ground several yards away. A small red light blinked from its underside and letters on one of the rotor arms spelled Mini2. *That's not a death ray.* Just some amateur trying to get footage of the soirée. And definitely not the cause of disintegrations. So who was attacking them and from where?

She turned a full circle, looking for a shooter as she dug out the cell phone she'd stashed in the bodice of her gown. She knew she shouldn't have listened to Georgie's insistence that a police uniform didn't fit the theme for participants in the dating auction. Trying to keep her curious dog from burying her nose in alien goo, she called dispatch.

An automated voice said, "All circuits are busy. Please try your call again later."

"Fuck." She shoved the phone back into her bodice and watched as women in ball gowns tripped over toppled chairs, loose pets, and each other in their need to flee.

Towering well above the crowd, a singular set of broad blue shoulders and flowing navy colored hair was moving toward the park's fountain. He appeared to be the only surviving blue alien at the party. Was he responsible for the attack—or trying to escape it?

Cursing silently at her four-inch heels, she followed him, threading between the abandoned tables. Pepper wanted to stop and sniff every toppled chair and discarded napkin, and she was forced to yank on the lead to make her obey. "Pepper, heel, or so help me—"

Overhead, a pair of helicopters came into view, spotlights panning the tables as they descended to the lawn behind the stage. Someone must've gotten the word to the authorities. But her intuition was tingling about the blue alien she'd seen fleeing.

She hurried along the path toward the fountain, following the string of lights hung between poles to make the evening more romantic. Poor Georgie must be beside herself over what was happening to her premier event.

Pepper spotted a loose dog and veered off the path, trying to drag Lora with her. Lora'd enrolled her in obedience school and had been training her to track scents, but the dog was willful beyond belief. "Damnit, not now." Lora gritted her teeth, keeping firm hold of the leash.

She looked back up to find the blue alien striding toward her. He was tall, towering over her despite the added height of her pumps. Suddenly realizing she had no weapon, no cuffs, not even a radio to call for help, she held up one palm. "Springfield Police Department. Freeze."

He stopped a few steps away. His well-muscled chest was bare, narrow hips clothed in blue jeans, and the light stubble of a beard dusted his jaw.

Her mouth went dry. She couldn't tell where his solid black eyes were focused, but despite the chaos around them, it felt like he was undressing her with his gaze. Unbidden curiosity about how that stubble might feel against the tender flesh of her thighs filled her. *Wrong moment, wrong guy, Lora.* But damn if he wasn't the sexiest man—alien or otherwise—she'd ever laid eyes on.

Curious as always, Pepper surged forward to greet the stranger.

The sudden change in trajectory made Lora stumble, ankle twisting in her heels. The leash was yanked from her grip and she tumbled forward, hands out to catch herself.

The alien somehow averted the dog and managed to catch Lora before she crashed to her knees. His big hands were warm on her bare arms, his naked blue chest right at eye level. *Damn.* He was ripped. He even smelled sexy, like warm spices with a hint of leather. Her knees suddenly felt weak from more than just the tumble she'd almost taken.

She lifted her gaze to meet his glittering dark eyes and swallowed. *Stand up, you idiot.* But her legs felt too wobbly to hold her weight.

"You are injured," he said. His voice had a smoky depth that shot straight to her core.

What was wrong with her? This guy was turning her into a slobbering idiot. At least he didn't seem to intend her any harm.

"I'll be fine. I just need to take these shoes off." Still leaning on his arm, she slid her injured foot out of the pump. But when she tried to put weight on it to remove her other shoe, pain rocketed through her ankle. She fell to one knee on the grass.

Pepper took that as in invitation to play and barreled into her, knocking her flat onto the ground. "Pepper, no! Stop."

God, could this be more embarrassing? She wrapped one arm around Pepper's neck to keep her under control and managed to push herself up to her knees, trying not to think about the grass stains she was probably getting on her expensive dress.

The alien suddenly stiffened, and she thought she was about to see another guy turn into goo. Instead, he lifted his arm, and a semi-transparent screen appeared above his wrist, just like in a sci-fi movie. Another alien's blue face floated in the air, speaking a language Lora didn't understand.

Then she heard a familiar voice. "Lora! Are you okay?"

"Georgie?" Lora let go of Pepper and grabbed the alien's outstretched arm, dragging herself upright onto her good foot. "Where are you?"

The big blue man frowned and pulled his arm from her grasp so the screen once more faced him. After a few more words with the other alien, the screen disappeared.

Lora reached for his arm again. "That was my friend! What have you done with her? What's going on?"

The alien tilted his head, as if taking a moment to understand. This close, she saw his eyes weren't completely black, but deep blue with no whites. His nose was slightly crooked, as if it had been broken at some point. "Your friend is safe. She's with Prince Arazhi."

"Prince?" Lora gaped. "What prince? What's going on?" She took a hobbling step forward and gritted her teeth against the pain lancing through her ankle.

Without warning, the alien swept her into his arms and strode toward the stage where the helicopters could be heard winding down. "Someone tried to assassinate the crown prince. I must find out who."

Lora clung to his neck. She wasn't exactly a small woman, but he carried her as if she weighed nothing. Before she could ask more questions, a man's voice called out, "Hey! You! Come with us."

Twisting her neck, she spotted a pair of men in black suits approaching along the path ahead. *Probably Feds.* And here she was being carried like a damsel in distress. The guys at the precinct were going to have a heyday when they heard about it.

She patted the alien's shoulder. "Put me down, please."

He hesitated, gaze concentrated on the men, then gently set her on her feet.

Keeping her weight on her good ankle, she reached into her bodice to retrieve her badge. "Springfield P—"

"Gun!" The shorter man shouted, drawing his pistol.

2

Zhiruto lunged past the human female and grabbed the man's weapon, forcing him to the ground. The only thing on his mind was protecting the female. *My female.*

The moment he'd touched her, he'd sensed she would be his perfect mate. The feeling had been so distracting, he'd missed his teleportation window off the planet. Now he was stuck here, protecting a female he neither knew nor owned, yet who'd captured his attention in the most primal way possible.

My mate.

The human male he now held pinned was leaking aggression like a Kryillian death swarm. The taller human with him was more nervous than hostile as he pulled his own weapon, so Zhiruto ignored him; if the man fired the primitive projectile, it would now be at Zhiruto, not the female, and a Kirenai's shapeshifting matrix could absorb the impact—he was certain the female's physiology could not.

"Stop!" the female shouted. "Don't hurt him!"

The universal translator was still updating, and Zhiruto wasn't sure if she was talking to him or the other men, but he kept his focus on the grappled man and spoke carefully, "I do not intend harm."

The taller human male spoke in a shaky voice, "Let him go. Now."

Zhiruto's Iki'i—his Kirenai empathic sense—itched with the emotions swirling around the humans. The female had said she was with the police, a human term he recognized as one of authority. He looked at her. "Shall I release him?"

She was clinging to a gold charm shaped like a primitive shield that hung around her neck. "Not yet." She turned her attention toward the taller male. "I don't know what sort of operation you're running, but I was trying to identify myself." She raised the charm. "Lora Griffin, Springfield P.D. Now who the fuck are you?"

A surge of jealousy rose in Zhiruto—she hadn't even bothered to ask his name when they'd met. He needed to remedy that immediately.

The man slowly lowered his weapon and pulled a black wallet from his jacket. "Agent Richfield. National Security."

Loragriffin took a limping step to look closer, making Zhiruto's possessiveness nearly consume him. He needed to get himself under control before his urges made him do something rash.

She examined the wallet, then nodded before looking once more at Zhiruto. "They're NSA. You can let him go."

Reluctantly, Zhiruto relaxed his grip and stepped back. The human he'd been holding scrambled to his feet and smoothed his hands over the lapels of his jacket. "The alien needs to come with us."

Zhiruto stiffened. He wasn't about to let this NSA—whatever that was—make him look like a nobody in front of Loragriffin. "I am Zhiruto Miru, head of security for Crown Prince Arazhi Yazhu. Take me to your leader immediately."

The shorter human let out a barking laugh. "Seriously?" He turned to the other man. "He just said take me to your leader."

"What's he supposed to say?" Loragriffin stepped in, as confident as a queen issuing a royal edict. "Just take us to whoever's in charge."

Zhiruto couldn't help but smile. She was magnificent.

The shorter man looked her up and down with unconcealed disdain, then glanced at Zhiruto before nodding. "This way."

Zhiruto yearned to put the man in his place, but Loragriffin called for something called "pepper" and emitted a whistle his translator couldn't interpret. *Is that how humans signal they're in pain?* Or perhaps pepper was an analgesic. He didn't have any painkillers on him, but he offered to carry her again.

She refused, continuing to call out as she limped after the man.

Appreciation of her strength rose up inside him. He'd noticed it earlier when she'd been on stage, and would've bid on her if he hadn't already purchased a female—not that he wanted to own a bondservant for himself. Empress Vella had given him orders to purchase a back-up female in case the reluctant prince failed to win one. He'd lost sight of his new bondservant during the chaos, but that no longer mattered. Now that he knew the prince had secured one of his own, Zhiruto would let her go.

He'd rather spend his time on Earth with Loragriffin.

The NSA men led them past the tables where fallen Kirenai lay puddled on the grass, dull blue and lifeless. None of the formless shapes near the tables appeared to be moving or attempting to reform, and Zhiruto's stomach churned with dismay. As shapeshifters, his people could assume the appearance of any species in the galaxy, but their natural state was an unformed cellular matrix which humans might associate with an amoeba. A Kirenai never used that form in public, but there were some toxins that could force them into it, most notably the poison which had recently weakened the emperor. Could this have been caused by the same poison? And why didn't the IDA have its healers out seeing to the fallen?

Well away from the tables, a cluster of humans and their accompanying quadrupeds stood near the stage surrounded by armed men in camouflage clothing. Several of the quadrupeds barked. Two females sobbed, while another spoke to the guards, demanding something she called a "cell phone." His universal translator was sending him conflicting interpretations of what the word "cell" meant, and he tapped the implant in his wrist, frustrated that humans had so many languages and idioms the translation database had yet to parse.

Loragriffin's quadruped appeared within the crowd, held in check by a female with obsidian hair and a burgundy gown. Relief wafted from Loragriffin. "Can you watch Pepper for a bit, Maise? I'm on duty."

The female called Maise replied, "Sure!"

Pepper is the name of her quadruped, Zhiruto realized.

When he'd first arrived on the planet, he'd assumed the furry mammals were in charge of the females, given the way the humans seemed to defer to them. But after he'd attempted to speak with one he'd realized the creatures were of lesser intelligence. Since human females had strong maternal instincts, he'd concluded that they must need the animals as surrogate children until they could be impregnated. Just the thought of impregnating Loragriffin made his human anatomy swell uncomfortably.

They continued on toward the pale yellow tent that had been used for food preparation. Now, two men in matching black suits blocked the entrance.

Loragriffin lifted her charm in front of their faces. "Springfield Police—"

"We'll take it from here," the shorter of their escorts interrupted. "You can join the others." He pointed back toward the humans near the stage.

"Now hold on..." She protested as a man in a camouflage uniform took her arm.

Zhiruto couldn't read thoughts, only sense emotion, and all he could read on the men at the moment was walled resolution. But Loragriffin didn't trust them, and that made Zhiruto suspicious, as well. He took her other arm. "The female comes with me."

"We've been instructed to segregate the aliens."

"This female has the authority of your police," Zhiruto insisted. "I require her aid."

Loragriffin shot him a surprised glance, and gratitude warmed his Iki'i. Zhiruto found he liked the sensation. *Don't let yourself be distracted*, he reminded himself, forcing his focus back to the guards. He had to get the situation under control and begin his hunt for the assassin—his prince's safety depended on it.

A man inside the tent said, "It's fine. Let them in."

Zhiruto pulled her inside. Glaring artificial lights cut across the tent from each corner, and the clunky food heating appliances were now shoved to one end. A group of humans stood around a table looking at folding data pads. Beyond them, a paltry pair of human-shaped Kirenai stood submissively under guard along with a pink-scaled Qalqan, the two Khargal guests, and the single Fogarian he recalled from the guest list.

A small measure of relief shuddered through him as he realized he wasn't the only Kirenai left standing.

The human who'd tried to shoot Loragriffin nudged him in the back, speaking toward a man with dark skin and close-cropped silver hair. "This one was wandering around the park."

Zhiruto focused on the dark-skinned man who was obviously in charge. "I am Zhiruto Miru, head of security for—"

The man held up a hand. "We're still coordinating a grounds sweep. Go wait over there with your friends and I'll get to you in a minute."

Zhiruto scowled. This human obviously didn't have a clue about what was happening. "Our healer needs to look for survivors."

"I said, over there. I have my people on it now."

Loragriffin pulled her arm from Zhiruto's grip and stepped up to the man, waving her charm. "Is this how the NSA trains its people to interact with foreign dignitaries? Not to mention he's talking about saving survivors, asshole—"

"I let you in here as a courtesy," the man growled. "If you can't keep a civil tongue, I'll have my men show you out."

The female continued arguing, but Zhiruto didn't have time to wait for the outcome. Loragriffin could obviously handle herself with these men, and he'd already allowed himself to be distracted by her when he should have been escorting his prince back to Kirenai Prime. Now his only task must be tracking down the assassin.

He turned toward the surviving guests at the back of the tent. The Qalqan healer was the head of first aid for the IDA. The Khargals and Fogarian were guests he recognized from the party. And both Kirenai wore IDA badges on white shirts they'd obviously acquired to appear more human; his own clothing was a mere mimicry of human garb.

"Have we checked for survivors?" he asked the healer.

The pink-scaled Qalqan shook his head. "I haven't been allowed a full triage, but the few I was able to scan were deceased." He gestured toward a dull blue matrix lying flat against the grass in the opposite corner of the tent. "That was the IDA's planetary manager. So far, it appears only Kirenai were affected."

Zhiruto's gut clenched. There had been almost twenty Kirenai guests on the list, plus another handful on the IDA staff.

He gestured to the remaining Kirenai. "So why are we still okay?"

"I believe the food was poisoned," said the healer. "Did you eat anything?"

Zhiruto shook his head, glad he hadn't sampled any of the human delicacies during his initial tour of the tent. Had his prince? Dread filled Zhiruto. He couldn't warn Prince Arazhi while the ship's FTL drive was engaged.

By the time the ship reached Kirenai Prime, it might be too late.

The taller Khargal fluttered his wings, as if wishing to take to the air. "I sampled the paltry meal and feel perfectly well. Why are we being held prisoner? I demand to be allowed to collect my female and depart this wretched planet immediately."

Zhiruto's Iki'i was swept by unease from the survivors. He gave the Khargal a hard stare. "Nobody's leaving until I have answers."

"You're Prince Arazhi's man, aren't you?" asked the other Khargal, wings furled tightly against his back. "Was the prince harmed?"

Zhiruto narrowed his eyes. As shapeshifters, his species could move among other species without revealing their true identities; only other Kirenai could discern one from another by using their Iki'i. Prince Arazhi had not used his public form—the one the rest of the galaxy would instantly recognize—during his visit to Earth. "How did you know the prince was here?"

"You introduced yourself to the 'humons' as Zhiruto Miru, and everyone knows you never leave Prince Arazhi's side," said the Khargal. "I met you with the prince at a ball on Vatosang."

He didn't recognize the Khargal; but then, he met a lot of people in his travels with the prince. Before answering, he opened his Iki'i for reactions, and he watched the Qalqan for shifts in body language as the species was immune to Iki'i sense. They were seldom involved in aggression, but Zhiruto wasn't willing to rule anyone out, not when there was a high probability the culprit was standing before him now.

He said, "The prince escaped the planet without injury."

Only relief touched his senses throughout the group, and even the Qalqan nodded in obvious relief. *The suspect isn't one of those here at the moment.* Which meant the culprit had either transported before the window closed or was loose on the planet somewhere. *Could the assassin be human?* That thought sent a chill into his gut.

The Fogarian said, "I'm glad to assist with the investigation."

"Thank you."

The dark-skinned NSA man strode over, a data pad in one hand. "Thank you for your cooperation. My name's Agent Randall. I've been in contact with your IDA representatives, and we're working on getting a shuttle in to pick you up."

Loragriffin stood among the other humans, arms crossed over her chest, a smug smile on her face. She thought she'd helped gain them freedom, but little did she know she may have also given the assassin a way to escape.

"You must not allow orbital traffic until I've finished my investigation," Zhiruto said. "This was an assassination attempt, and the culprit is most likely still among us."

The belligerent Khargal groaned.

The Qalqan made a hissing sound. "Excuse me, but if there are any survivors among the fallen, they will need to be taken to the ship's medical bay right away."

Zhiruto ground his teeth. Finding the assassin was important, but so was saving lives. There was also a possibility one of the victims had seen something.

"Our medics confirmed all the, uh, remains we've found are dead," Agent Randall said.

"Your healers aren't equipped to deal with our medical requirements," Zhiruto replied. "Please allow us to see to the victims immediately."

Agent Randall's nose wrinkled, but then he nodded. "All right, go ahead. My men are available to help if you need them."

The Qalqan gathered his scanner and scurried from the tent, followed closely by three of the other agents.

Zhiruto slid his gaze to Loragriffin. He needed to speak with the humans who may have seen something, and to do that, he'd need help. "I would like your assistance speaking with the human guests."

Agent Randall started to protest. "She doesn't have clearance—"

"She's the only one I trust."

The man's jaw worked like he wanted to spit, then he shifted his eyes toward her. "I suppose she can be your liaison. Be sure to file a report with us as well as your precinct, Officer Griffin. Understand?"

Wide-eyed, she nodded. "Yes, sir."

Zhiruto hadn't known his request for her help would please her so much, but he felt himself swell with satisfaction. "Come, then." He gestured for her to precede him out of the tent.

3

*L*ora understood Agent Randall's not so subtle hint that she was now working for the NSA, and she wasn't sure how to feel about that. On one hand, it could lead to a promotion or even a new job with the Feds if she performed well. On the other, they were treating the aliens as if they were terrorists instead of the victims of the attack. It was a massive load of bullshit, and if she could help Zhiruto get to the bottom of these deaths, she would.

Trying to hide her limp, she exited the tent ahead of the tall blue alien. As she passed the small agent who'd pulled the gun on her, he muttered, "You've got no business being here."

Zhiruto halted midstep and turned a baleful glare at the man, sending him scurrying back inside.

Lora was really beginning to like Zhiruto, but she couldn't allow him to keep stepping in on her behalf. She put a hand on his arm, surprised by how human his blue skin felt under her palm. "Thanks, but I can fight my own battles."

He gave her a startled look. "You're going to battle?"

She grinned, picturing herself knocking the agent on his ass in kickboxing. She was pretty good in the ring, but she was certain the guy probably had some sort of special ops training a regular cop like her didn't have. Plus, her ankle was currently on fire. "It's just a figure of speech."

"I see." He turned toward the people gathered under the lights near the stage. "This is why I need your help communicating with the humans, Loragriffin."

"Just Lora. Please." It was nice to be appreciated, but his continued use of her name smashed together like that was beginning to feel awkward.

"Lora." He smiled. "A good name for you. It means 'persuasive' in Kirenai."

She had to smile, too. Persuasive sounded a lot more complimentary than the names she was usually called.

As they moved along the line of police tape cordoning off the tables, she watched the pink alien bend over a dark spot on the grass. He was waving what looked like a baton. "What's he doing?"

"Scanning for life signs."

She raised her eyebrows. The jelly-like splotches looked beyond help. Then again, she'd heard rumors the aliens had teleported down to Earth instead of landing in a ship, so maybe they had technology to perform reconstruction. "Can you resuscitate someone who's been disintegrated like that?"

He stopped walking and turned to her. "They were not disintegrated. They were denatured."

"What's the difference?"

He rubbed his chin, the stubble making scratchy noise under his fingers. Was it possible he'd gotten more handsome, or was she just desperate to get laid? It'd been quite a while since she'd been on a date, let alone taken a guy home. She usually preferred her vibrator over the entanglements of bringing a man into her life.

Zhiruto gestured toward a bench on the nearby trail. "If you are going to help me speak to these women, then I must first brief you on the situation."

She sank gratefully onto the bench and he settled down beside her. They were close but not touching, and every inch of her skin seemed hyper aware of his presence. It didn't help that he was still shirtless, his smooth bare chest and abs cut with muscles that flexed with his every move. She worked out at a gym every day with bodybuilders, and not a single one of them could compete with this guy.

Realizing she'd been staring at his perfect little nipples—a darker blue than the rest of his skin—she looked up to find him smiling like a Cheshire cat. *Shit, way to make a fool of yourself.* She planted one hand on the bench and nonchalantly leaned away from him. "So, what about denaturing or whatever?"

He imitated her posture, leaning the other way, which only made his torso seem that much more ripped. "First let me tell you about the emperor's son, Prince Arazhi."

She nodded, trying hard to keep her attention on his face. "The person you work for?"

"Yes. He's the heir to the Yazhu dynasty. His father is ill, and Prince Arazhi will soon take the throne."

"Let me guess. Somebody out there doesn't want that to happen." Overhead, a helicopter circled the night sky, while in the distance a babbling rumble told her a crowd had likely gathered at the park barricades. How much more chaotic would it get once people found out royalty was involved?

"Correct. There is a strong consortium of merchants within the Senburu—our confederation of planets—

who oppose the emperor's long-standing trade edicts. They've put forth their own candidate for the throne, and if Prince Arazhi can't produce an heir in the near future, it's likely they will enact a coup and seize power. That's why he came to Earth, to purchase a female to impregnate."

Lora sat up, horror chilling down her spine. Georgie was currently flying to God knew where on an alien spaceship with an alien who wanted to impregnate her. "Back up. Purchase? Are you saying he thinks Georgie is his slave?"

He tilted his head, as if trying to understand. "He purchased her contract. Did you not sell yourself as a bondservant, as well?"

"Definitely not." She stood, heart thundering against her ribs as she looked down at him. "The auction was for charity. You were bidding on a date, not a woman."

"Yes, a date. This means the delivery of viable bondservants."

She gulped. "There's been a mistake. That's not what dating means on Earth. It means spending time getting to know someone."

"I see." He rose. "This is an unfortunate misunderstanding. I'll see that our universal translator is updated."

"You need to call the prince back and clear this up right now."

"Agreed. However, they are out of communication range while they are traveling to Kirenai Prime. Please rest assured, Prince Arazhi won't harm your friend or force himself on her once he learns of the mistake. But he is short on time to sire an heir. I must ensure he has an alternative." He took a half-step backward, staring at her as if torn. "Would you be willing to have his child?"

She gaped at him. "What the hell? I've never even met him."

"So that is a no?"

"An emphatic no."

He nodded, and she thought he almost looked relieved. Turning toward the cluster of guarded women, he said, "Then let's go talk to the other females."

Thank God he gave up on the baby-making suggestion quickly. He most likely didn't see her as the motherly type. She was simply the first woman presented, and he'd be asking every woman the same question. She shoved aside the odd sense of disappointment threading through her chest. "I'm here to help you find a killer, not find the prince a date."

"Of course." Reaching out, he took her hand and put it on his arm. "Let's proceed with our questioning so everyone can go home."

She didn't want to look like she was being escorted to prom, but she was really feeling the swelling in her ankle, so she gave in and leaned on him to limp toward the group. The NSA guard handed Zhiruto a tablet. "This is a list of human guests. We're still tracking down a few."

"Thank you." Zhiruto passed her the device.

Lora accepted it, and the guard stepped aside to let them pass, body rigid and eyes following their progress like he was watching a snake slither past.

The women, however, were far less suspicious. They surged forward, questions flying from all directions. "What happened? Can we go home now? Are we under attack?"

Maise pushed to the front, multiple leashes clutched in her fists. As usual, she'd assumed responsibility for every stray dog she could find. She now held not only Pepper and her own dog, Floof, but an enormous Great Dane with striking blue eyes and a caramel-colored labradoodle.

Seeing Pepper again soothed Lora's frazzled nerves, and she rubbed the dog's ears. "Thanks for watching her. Thank you can keep an eye on her a bit longer?"

"Sure. Any idea who these belong to?" Maise gestured toward the other dogs in her care. The hem of her burgundy skirt was torn, and her raven curls had come loose from the messy bun she'd worn for the event.

"Sorry, no." The last thing on Lora's mind was tracking down missing dog owners. She turned to the crowd, most of whom she recognized from the pre-auction briefing. "Thank you for your patience, everyone."

She glanced at Zhiruto to find a brunette in a sequined black dress rubbing herself all over him. Well, all right, maybe not rubbing herself, but definitely clinging as if she knew him. Wanted him.

The woman said, "I'm so glad you're all right."

A flare of jealousy made Lora press her lips tightly together. *This must be the woman he thought he was buying at the auction.*

Zhiruto extracted his arm from the woman's grip. "I'm glad you're also unharmed. But in light of recent events, I must nullify our contract. Please step back with the others now."

A hurt look flitted across the woman's face, and she dropped her hands.

Lora's jealousy turned to pity as the woman slunk back to the others. Apparently the guy didn't know how to let someone down easy. But at least he was keeping to business, and she had to approve of that.

He looked at her and said, "Please proceed."

Lora nodded, considering how much to tell the women. She didn't want to fall into the weeds about the whole slavery issue; it wasn't like the aliens in question were in any state to claim ownership, anyway. The important thing right now was finding the killer.

She met the eyes of a woman holding a corgi, then shifted her attention among the women as she spoke. "I know tonight was traumatic, and we appreciate all of you remaining calm. I've been informed that this was an assassination attempt on an alien prince."

Collectively, all eyes turned toward Zhiruto, and the brunette edged a step forward. "You're a prince?"

This time, Lora's jealousy rose burning hot. "No. He's the prince's bodyguard."

Lascivious murmurs about sexy bodyguards forced her to speak louder so she'd be heard. "Ladies, please. Have some respect. Aliens have died and we need your help. Did anyone see anything unusual tonight?"

"More unusual than my date dissolving into a puddle right before my eyes?" asked the woman with the corgi.

Lora put on a stoic face. Even she had to admit she'd been pretty focused on her date when everything went down. "We'd like to speak to everyone individually about the events this evening."

"After that, can we go home?" asked an older woman in a puffy pink gown that looked like it had been a bridesmaid's dress in the eighties.

A scratchy shout came from the area of the tables, making everyone turn.

The pink alien was waving a wand in the air, and the three NSA medics were struggling to push a round cart with a portable MRI scanner across the grass.

"What's going on?" asked Lora.

Zhiruto was already stepping over the police tape. "They've found a survivor."

Lora's stomach flip-flopped, then she limped quickly after him, hoping she wasn't about to see a zombie arm sticking out of one of the blue globs.

4

Zhiruto strode over to the healer, heartened by news of a survivor. The healer was using an anti-gravity field generator to lift the Kirenai's cellular matrix from where it had collapsed on top of a chair. The two IDA representatives were trying to get a hovering transportation creche past the NSA men and their wheeled cart, and a handful of NSA humans crowded around the healer, more curious than helpful as they asked questions. Not only were they in the way, but a Kirenai's resting state was private. This victim deserved dignity.

Holding out his arms as if to block their view, Zhiruto said, "I must ask you to back away so our healer can work."

Agent Randall scowled. "I'm tired of you aliens always treating us as servants. This is an investigation on human soil. We need to be sure there's no threat to our own population."

Zhiruto moved in front of the man, arms crossed. "Is it common practice for your ancillary personnel to gawk at naked human victims? Because right now, this Kirenai is basically naked."

The man had the grace to emit remorse, though his scowl remained. "At least allow us to perform an MRI."

"We have no need of your scanner," said the healer. "Please move your people out of the way." He pointed toward the incoming transportation creche; the organic polymer box was of Qalqan design and would adjust its size to fit the occupant. It would also induce stasis until the appropriate medical facilities could be reached.

Agent Randall glanced at the creche then at Lora, who now stood a polite distance away before telling his men, "Everyone, back to your duties."

To their credit, the men didn't so much as grumble as they stepped away, but Zhiruto could still feel their curious eyes on the scene as they pretended to perform other duties nearby.

Agent Randall took several generous steps backward and continued watching, obviously not considering himself ancillary. There was a sense of avarice coming from him that Zhiruto didn't like, but it was one he'd encountered before—less advanced species often hoped to acquire new technology when they saw it. At least the agent was no longer in the healer's way.

Lora was obviously curious about the fallen Kirenai as well but stayed back.

He signaled her to join him.

She edged closer until she stood beside him, her bare shoulder brushing his arm, and watched the healer transfer the other Kirenai into a transportation creche. Amazement and pity brushed his Iki'i, mimicking his own emotions. That this Kirenai had survived where so many others had not was a miracle. It might also be a curse if the poison couldn't be purged; to be forever relegated to one's resting state would be a terrible fate.

Zhiruto searched for the survivor's Iki'i signature while the healer floated the unformed matrix upward and into the creche. He could sense the victim was alive, but this individual wasn't familiar to him. As the poisoned Kirenai settled inside the creche, the matrix shuddered, convulsed, and pulled into a human-looking face, only to subside once more into a gelatinous resting state.

Lora stumbled backward, wide eyes on the fallen Kirenai. "Holy shit, it *is* alive."

Although Lora's incredulity was strong, the victim's indignation was stronger, almost blinding in its intensity. Zhiruto pulled her aside and leaned close to her ear. "First of all, we say 'he' not 'it'. Second, he can hear you."

Eyebrows drawing together in horror, she nodded. "Oh, God. Sorry. He."

He smiled gently. "It wasn't a reprimand, only a correction. Humans are new to the galactic consortium. We have a lot to learn about each other."

"Is he in pain?"

Now that she mentioned it, Zhiruto was struck by the lack of pain he was sensing. Perhaps the poison also had a numbing effect. "No. He's just unable to rise from his resting state."

"Resting state? What's that?"

Although few had seen it, nearly everyone in the galaxy knew about the Kirenai resting state. "Did the IDA not brief you about the guests? Kirenai are shapeshifters, but we must occasionally allow our cellular matrix to relax."

She gaped, and her attention slid over his body. "You mean this isn't what you normally look like?"

"I can assume the shape of many species, although I'm always this color. I've simply assumed a shape pleasing to... humans." He didn't want to admit that much of what he looked like now—from his crooked nose to the stubble on his chin—was made for her pleasure.

"You're definitely going to need to give me more details on that later." She shook her head, gaze still roaming his chest. "After you finish here."

He nodded, pleased by how quickly she'd overcome her shock and focused back on the job. "I'll be more than happy to tell you more later." Returning his attention to the healer, he asked, "Do you have an ID for the victim?"

The Kirenai kept a genetic database to help track its population, since a Kirenai resumed his resting state upon death and would be unidentifiable any other way. The healer didn't look away from his task. "I will need to get him back to the ship to run a check."

Zhiruto moved forward, extending a hand toward the Kirenai's matrix; his species could share information through their Iki'i when they touched, even in their resting state. He'd simply ask the victim himself.

The healer placed a clawed hand on Zhiruto's arm to stop him. "Don't touch him until I determine if the cause of the condition is transmissible."

That brought Zhiruto up short. "I thought you said it was poison?"

"The poison could transfer between you if you attempt to interface with him."

Zhiruto let out a heavy sigh and dropped his hand. "All right. Just give me a few minutes before you put him into stasis."

Bowing slightly, the healer stepped back to wait. "Please proceed, but keep in mind that the longer he remains unstable, the more difficult it will be to recover."

Moving as close to the creche as possible without touching it, Zhiruto said, "My name's Zhiruto and I serve Prince Arazhi. I'm looking for the person who did this to you. Do you have any information about what happened?"

Anger shot against him like sharp needles along with a sense of affirmation.

Zhiruto's pulse picked up. *He does know something.* The urge to reach into the creche and get the information was difficult to resist. Without touching, he had to rely on yes or no questions. "Was it one of the Khargals?"

Negativity flowed to him.

"The Fogarian?"

Again, negativity.

He had difficulty believing a Kirenai could commit such an atrocity to their own kind, so he asked, "A human?"

A human-looking face formed once more in the matrix, and a single word escaped the Kirenai's lips. "*Burendo.*"

Zhiruto stiffened as the Kirenai relaxed into his resting state once more. All Kirenai could change shape, but *burendo* could change color, as well, and could blend into local populations almost as well as the natives. It meant the culprit was not only Kirenai, but had likely escaped into hiding among the billions of humans here on the planet. And if the *burendo* was a trained assassin, he'd know how to shield himself from another's Iki'i as well. *How am I going to track him down now?*

"What did he say?" whispered Lora, touching his arm.

He gestured for the healer to proceed with sealing the creche—there was nothing more he needed from the victim. Then he turned to Lora. "*Burendo.* It's a Kirenai who can change color and shape. They're extremely rare."

"So the murderer is one of these *burendo*?" Her gaze slid toward a nearby NSA guard. "He or she could look exactly like a human?"

Zhiruto hadn't even had time to consider the assassin could be mimicking not only a human, but a female.

Kirenai were an all-male species, but were still capable of assuming a female form if they so desired.

His job had grown exponentially more impossible.

He looked at the gathered humans pressing against the boundary set by the NSA guards. "Do you know these humans personally?"

"A lot of them, yes. Are you suggesting one of them may be a—a doppelgänger?"

His translator took a moment to interpret the word. When it did, he shook his head. "A *burendo* can't assume the look of a specific individual very well, and wouldn't know how to imitate that person without extensive study. Normally, I could detect another Kirenai's Iki'i, but an assassin is likely shielding himself while I'm around. However, if you know these women, I believe it should be easy to confirm each is who she says she is."

She nodded. "All right." Her gaze flicked toward Agent Randall hovering nearby. "But don't tell Randall about the *burendo* or he'll freak out and these women will never make it home. The last thing you want is the NSA to take over. We'd be buried in all sorts of testing and red tape."

Zhiruto didn't know what red tape meant, but he trusted Lora's judgment. "Let's not mention it to anyone. If the assassin finds out we know what he is, he'll be more cautious."

"Good point," Lora said. "Let's make this *burendo* feel comfortable, and perhaps they'll slip up."

He liked that their minds followed the same path. Smiling, he nodded at his partner. "Let's go speak to your friends."

5

$\mathcal{L}$ora was to return to the gathered women and begin questioning them while Zhiruto went to check on the status of the incoming shuttle. She stopped by the restroom on her way over, thinking about everything she'd learned. Zhiruto was not only an alien, he was a shapeshifter. But the hard-muscled blue man she'd been drooling over was nothing like a werewolf in the books she enjoyed. He was actually more like a creature from *The Blob*. *He looks and feels so real*. Hell, he even smelled real, like the best masculine cologne she could imagine. When she thought about it, a shapeshifting blob wasn't really that much more fantastical than a werewolf. Just a bit less cuddly. The thought made her laugh.

She stepped out of the restroom and limped toward the stage. The sky had begun lightening toward the east,

42

and the women all looked haggard and exhausted in their rumpled evening gowns. Even the dogs looked ready to go home, no longer playing or barking, just lying around sleeping or watching their owners with sad eyes.

The women perked up when Lora passed between the guards. Several rushed over and began babbling questions as she approached. "Is one still alive? Are we suspects? Why are they keeping us here?"

She had to use her hard-ass police voice to get them to calm down. "Sit down and be quiet or none of us will be getting out of here anytime soon. To answer your questions, yes, one of the aliens is still alive. He's being taken to their medical facility." She decided to refrain from going into the whole "resting state" thing; it would only cause more questions. "Now if you'll please cooperate, I'm going to try to clear you all to go home."

That got a collective sigh of relief and the ladies trudged back to their seats.

Maise remained standing, three dogs on leashes standing around her like sentinels plus Pepper, who was now whining at the sight of Lora.

"Thanks for hanging onto her. I can take her back now." Lora took the leash, bending down to let Pepper nuzzle her ear. It felt good to have her dog back. She glanced up at Maise, taking in her bleary eyes and drooping bun of black hair. "Why don't I talk to you first?"

Several women grumbled about playing favorites, but Lora ignored them and led the way to one end of the stage where two chairs sat on the grass next to a table that had once held champagne.

Glad to take the weight off her ankle, she sat, tying Pepper to the back of her chair while Maise looped the leashes of the other three dogs on a railing at the edge of the stage. Grabbing two bottled waters from a nearby table, Maise joined her, handing one over. "I haven't seen Georgie since this all happened. Do you know where she is?"

Lora rubbed the back of her neck. "She's, ah, with the prince, I guess."

"Get outta town." Maise's eyes widened. "Where are they? When do I get to meet him?"

"They're on a spaceship, I think. I saw her briefly when Zhiruto Facetimed them or whatever aliens call it."

"A spaceship?" Maise gasped. "Is she okay?"

"Yeah, I think so. At least, Zhiruto says she's not in danger."

Maise gave Lora a scrutinizing look. "I thought you were on official police duty, but you keep mentioning Zhiruto. Is that your alien bodyguard?"

Suddenly reminded of the feel of Zhiruto's muscles and his warm masculine scent when he'd carried her, Lora flushed. "He's not my bodyguard. He's the prince's. And I'm working for the NSA as a liaison."

"A liaison, huh?" Maise smirked. "Leading an investigation with a hot shirtless guy is probably like a dream date for you."

Lora crossed her arms. "Zhiruto isn't my date, and I'm not leading the investigation. Plus, there are more than a dozen dead aliens only footsteps away. Definitely not a dream date or the time to be thinking of hot guys."

"You're right." Maise stopped smirking and dropped her gaze. "This entire thing is awful."

Lora nodded, feeling like a hypocrite—she'd been thinking about how hot Zhiruto was all evening. "Let's get on with a few questions so I can let you go home, okay?"

Maise nodded.

"Does everyone here seem normal to you?" Keeping the *burendo* a secret was going to make asking questions more difficult. At least she was already certain Maise was really who she claimed to be. "I'm looking for anyone who seemed less shocked than they should be. Or more shocked. Anything strange at all."

Maise thought a second. "I think people are acting pretty normal. Heather's been crying non-stop. Meg's her usual bossy self. I suppose Tammy's been a little quieter than usual, but I think she's in shock. Someone said she and her date were kissing when it happened. She got blue goo all over her when he dissolved, and the NSA confiscated her dress."

Lora shuddered and glanced toward where Tammy sat with her knees drawn up to her chest, wearing nothing but a thin slip with a gray wool blanket draped over her shoulders. "Damn."

"You should probably talk to her next so she can get out of here. I think a bunch of us will need counseling after tonight."

"Thanks, Maise. I'll let the guards know you're clear to leave."

Maise rose and gathered the dogs. "I'm going to take these two to the shelter. Let me know if you talk to anyone missing their dogs."

"You bet."

Lora had just finished questioning Tammy when Zhiruto returned. The poor woman had stuttered her way through the questions, but she was also very clearly the same woman Lora'd met a few times while volunteering at the shelter. She instructed one of the guards to call Tammy a cab as Zhiruto held out a paper cup.

"The humans in the tent are all drinking this," he said. "I thought you might like some." The dark, rich scent of hot coffee wafted from its open top.

"God, yes, thank you." she said, taking a grateful sip. He'd even managed to douse it with the right amount of cream and sugar. She was used to pulling late shifts as a cop, but not without coffee. She closed her eyes with pleasure as the caffeine burned down her throat.

Zhiruto made a small noise that sounded almost like a growl, and her eyes popped back open to find him staring at her with a hungry expression.

Her throat tightened. "Do you, uh, want a taste?"

"More than you know."

She instantly knew he wasn't talking about the coffee, and desire flushed through her, centering deep in her core. She almost couldn't breathe with its intensity.

Focus on the job, you dingbat, she told herself. She had guys come onto her all the time, and brushing them off was second nature. But then, very few of them were built like Zhiruto. Swallowing, she set the coffee aside and turned her eyes to the list of attendees on the iPad the NSA had given her. "Let's stick to business. We have a lot more people to process, so we'd better keep moving."

Zhiruto pulled a chair over from a nearby table and sat. "Please continue. I appreciate your help."

Pepper put her head on Zhiruto's lap and he patted the top of her skull uncertainly. Pepper whined louder.

"Pepper, stop bothering him and go lay down."

"The quadruped isn't bothering me, Loragriffin. She will lie down in a moment."

More tingly feelings raced through Lora as she watched his big hand smooth over Pepper's sleek red fur. Damn, she was a sucker for a guy with a dog. Shaking it off, she called the next person over, trying hard to focus on her questions instead of the towering masculinity next to her.

The rest of the interviews went quickly as the sky above the trees to the east went from pale violet to the gold of sunrise, and the faint whine of morning traffic joined the chorus of birds in the trees. She had little trouble determining that the people she spoke with were who they said they were, mostly by using questions about the animal shelter. A freckled young man with bloodshot eyes who'd been one of the servers gave her a moment of panic when he stuttered out a nonsensical answer about how he'd landed the job, but then she realized it was because he'd lied about being twenty-one.

"I d-didn't touch the champagne. Not even to serve it. I swear."

She handed him back his driver's license. "I'm letting you go this time because we have bigger things to track down. But if we catch you again, you're in trouble. Now go home."

"Yes, officer." The young man stumbled off.

She turned to Zhiruto. "That's everyone on my list except Georgie and someone named Malorie Schmidt."

"We're handling the missing women." Agent Randall's voice behind her chair made her startle. He stepped into view with three guards behind him. "I've sent agents to their homes and work. From here on out, this is a classified operation. Time for you to go, officer."

Zhiruto rose. "Her assistance is still required. I must find the assassin."

"She's been helpful clearing the civilians, but this is non-negotiable. The order comes from the President himself." Randall speared her with bloodshot eyes. "My men will escort you to your vehicle."

Lora knew better than to argue. She'd only end up in jail, and she'd be zero help in there. "It's okay, Zhiruto. I'll check in on Malorie." She pulled out her cell phone and removed a business card from the slot on the back, handing it to Zhiruto. "Here's my contact information if you need to reach me."

He stared at her with an unfathomable expression that somehow made her chest ache, and she realized this could be the last time she ever saw him. As strange as it was, she wished they were alone so she could kiss him goodbye. *This wasn't a date, Lora,* she told herself. Hell, he probably didn't even find her attractive—after all, he'd bid on another woman.

She held out her hand. "It was an honor working with you, Zhiruto. Sorry your first visit to our planet was a disaster."

"I will contact you, Loragriffin. Thank you for your help."

The way he said he'd contact her made her stomach flutter. She nodded and turned to leave, recalling how Maise had teased her that this had been Lora's dream date. *I really hope he calls me,* she thought. But then again, she wasn't even sure he had a cell phone.

6

Zhiruto didn't like the way Agent Randall's men escorted Loragriffin away as if she were nothing more than a stray *ijin'en*, but Agent Randall was clearly finished accommodating Zhiruto's investigation. The man pointed toward the tent. "Your healer says he's completed his scans and there are no more survivors. You need to wait with your compatriots until the ship arrives."

"The assassin may have escaped your park." Zhiruto shot back, his gaze flicking distastefully to the NSA personnel pushing a cart carrying their rudimentary scanning equipment toward another victim. No wonder the emperor had wanted to give Earth more time to mature before opening its borders—the people in charge had no respect for other cultures. "I must be allowed to find him."

"We're handling it. We've got the city on lockdown and we're searching all outbound traffic." Agent Randall glanced over Zhiruto's body. "He can't hide long looking like one of you."

Zhiruto opened his mouth to explain that the assassin could just as easily look human, then recalled Loragriffin's warning not to tell Randall about the *burendo*. He'd gotten to know not only Loragriffin better during the interviews, but her friends, as well. The women had gone safely home, and he didn't want to say something that would cause them pointless trouble. Yet he also couldn't allow the NSA to end his investigation.

He looked at the card Loragriffin had given him. He didn't need it to locate her—he could tap into Earth's interweb database for that—but it was the only thing he had of her if he never saw her again. And he really wanted to see her again. *I could use her help for the investigation,* he thought as Agent Randall nudged him toward the tent.

The smell of death permeated the air inside, and the remaining off-planet guests stood or sat stiffly in one corner, as far from the flattened blue remains of the IDA's planetary manager as possible. The transportation creche holding the survivor hovered at the opposite side next to the healer, its clear rounded walls revealing the murky blue matrix of the Kirenai inside. Multicolored lights winked from the interface on top.

"There's been a small delay getting your ship cleared to land, but we'll get you out of here soon," Agent Randall said in a falsely friendly tone. "Everyone hang tight."

Hang tight sounded like a threat to Zhiruto, but the agent returned to his group of humans without further remark. Zhiruto sighed and went to stand next to the healer. Speaking in Qalqan, he asked, "How is the surviving victim?"

"Stable. I'll have a more reliable prognosis once we get him back to the IDA medical bay."

Zhiruto nodded. "Everyone else feeling all right?"

The taller Khargal stepped forward, furled wings jutting sharply above his shoulders. "I want my female. The humans have overridden my bondservant contract and freed her."

Khargals could get aggressive when it came to females; it would be best to clear up the misconception before things escalated. "I lost my bondservant, as well," Zhiruto commiserated, though he was glad that tie was severed. He'd much rather spend his time on Earth with Loragriffin. "There seems to have been a cultural misunderstanding about the auction. The females were selling something they call a 'date'—an evening of their company—not a bondservant contract."

"What?" the Khargal roared, spinning to glare at the nearest IDA representative. "My introductory documents clearly stated this was a bondservant auction."

The smaller Kirenai tapped his wrist to bring up an interface, reciting a rote response. "Here is the clause at the end of the contract that excuses the IDA from any unforeseen cultural misunderstandings."

The Khargal brought his rock-like fists up, looking ready to pummel the IDA employee into the ground.

The last thing they needed was a fight. The humans would probably try to separate them at the first sign of violence, and Zhiruto needed everyone's help to get him out of here. "We can take that up with the IDA after we get off the planet. Right now, I need to get away from these humans so I can continue my investigation."

"Whatever I can do," the offending IDA representative said, and everyone but the enraged Khargal nodded.

Zhiruto stepped closer to the Khargal. "Once this is over, I will see that the prince recognizes each of you for your help."

The Khargal snarled, but grumbled something Zhiruto's Iki'i understood as agreement.

Running a pink claw over the length of his portable scanner, the healer said, "The humans do not seem capable of detecting life in a Kirenai matrix. Perhaps you could enact your death by entering your resting state. Then the agents would no longer be concerned with your whereabouts."

Zhiruto recalled the way the agents outside were poking and prodding the Kirenai remains. "They're examining the dead fairly closely. I think they'd notice if I dropped dead then went missing."

The Fogarian cleared his throat, running a hand down one bushy red sideburn. "Forgive me, but all dead Kirenai look alike." He looked toward the dead Kirenai in the corner. "If you were to enter your resting state over the top of one, the humans might not notice when you broke away."

Revulsion filled Zhiruto's throat at the thought of mingling with the matrix of a fellow Kirenai, but the plan had merit. He turned to the healer. "Have you determined if the poison is transmissible?"

"Not yet." The healer shook his head. "However, I could place a temporary static barrier over the remains that should keep your matrices separate. Give me a few moments."

Zhiruto followed the healer toward the remains. The sour odor of the dead Kirenai wafted toward him as the healer circled his wand over its gelatinous surface. Leaving the park on his own might not be the best idea, but he also couldn't afford to be locked away with the others.

"The field is in place now," said the healer.

"Thank you." Zhiruto reached out and touched the matrix. The faint, cold sensation of the static field met his fingertips. Even so, he hoped he didn't have to remain in contact long.

He glanced toward the humans at the front of the tent. One of the guards watched him without expression, but Zhiruto could feel twinges of curiosity coming from him. The discussion about the plan had been in Qalqan, so he wasn't worried about the humans catching on, but he did want more eyes on him so the humans would have no doubt about what happened. Roaring as if in pain, he let his cellular matrix come undone and collapsed forward onto the remains, drawing himself into a flat denseness to minimize his size.

The guard shouted for assistance, and Agent Randall along with several more humans rushed over.

A Kirenai's hearing and vision were less refined while in a resting state, but Zhiruto could see the blurry form of the healer blocking the humans. "I warned him the poison might be transferable if he touched the remains." The healer waved his scanner. "But he insisted."

Agent Randall shoved his hands on his hips, the toes of his boots nearly touching Zhiruto's flattened matrix. He was uttering a string of human curse words related to excrement and procreation. "Get our fucking MRI machine in here now! I want every scrap of data we can gather."

Zhiruto remained unmoving, though every fiber of his being wanted to squirm away. The healer made a few useless attempts to stop the humans from using their machines.

Agent Randall had him escorted back to the other side of the tent. "Stay out of our way. If whatever's causing this is transmissible, I need to make sure it can't spread to humans."

"I assure you, it cannot—" the healer tried to protest.

But Agent Randall called several more guards into the tent, cordoning the healer and the others off from where Zhiruto now lay.

Remaining still, Zhiruto endured many needles piercing his matrix as well as extended magnetic scans, despite the healer's attempts to stop them. Growing increasingly impatient, he waited as the sun passed its zenith. Darkness was approaching by the time the humans admitted that they could find no life signs.

Agent Randall rounded on the remaining group. "No one goes anywhere or touches anything else until you're back on your ship and out of here. I don't need any more mishaps on human soil."

He strode from the tent. The other humans returned to their data pads, and the guards once more assumed watch over the IDA guests.

Slowly, Zhiruto eased his cellular matrix beneath the nearby table and toward the wall of the tent, slipping beneath the edge into the grass outside. The breeze had picked up, and the yellow fabric puffed and billowed like a great beast trying to swallow him. The humans had glaring lights set up across the park, and the short blades of foliage provided little cover. Stretching himself long and thin, he flowed along the tent's perimeter toward the far corner where the shadows were deepest, keeping his Iki'i alert for anyone nearby.

He flowed as quickly as he could toward the trees, continuing through the underbrush until he reached a woven wire fence. On the other side, the land was divided by more fences separating what appeared to be a line of human domiciles. Though it was dark, many of the humans were not only awake, but outside, sitting on chairs in the grass or strolling on the street which ran alongside the buildings.

Zhiruto needed to resume his human form so he could call Loragriffin, but the one thing Agent Randall had right was that blending into the human population would be impossible for normal Kirenai. He eased along the fence, skirting a barking quadruped that radiated deep aggression. When he reached a quiet domicile, he entered along a wooden fence and pulled himself into his human form.

A wall of fluttering cloth stretched between two posts near the building, and it took Zhiruto a moment to realize it was clothing. He had no idea why someone would string clothing like that, and he hoped he wasn't defiling a sacred ritual as he yanked a gray short-sleeved shirt free. Though it hadn't been raining, the fabric was wet and had a pleasant scent.

He pulled the shirt over his head and looked down his front, comparing his emulated blue slacks to a pair of gray ones hanging from the line. *Might as well use everything available.* He jerked the pants from the line, reforming his legs to slide the uncomfortably wet fabric up around his hips.

Most of him looked human now, but not well enough to walk in free view of the humans. A square of yellow fabric printed with pink, long-eared creatures hung with the clothing, and he used it to cover his head and shoulders. He hadn't seen any humans cover their heads like this, but then he also hadn't seen any with blue hair. At least this fabric was human.

Tapping the microchip embedded in his arm, he brought up his comm interface and contacted Loragriffin.

ora was dreaming of big blue hands running over her skin when her cell phone rang. Groaning, she opened her eyes and groped for the phone. The incoming number was blocked.

"Fuckin' A," she swore, dropping the phone and rolling over. She'd spent the morning at the precinct filling out reports, then went to check on Malorie—who'd already been picked up by the NSA—before being called in to help with a domestic altercation at one of the many alien welcome parties going on around town. By the time she got home, she'd barely managed to take a shower before dropping into bed like a log.

A muffled voice drifted toward her from the sheets where she'd dropped the phone. "Loragriffin, are you there?"

She sat bolt upright. "Zhiruto?"

At the foot of the bed, Pepper groaned and stretched.

Lora located the phone and turned it over. Zhiruto's face looked back at her from the screen—she must've accidentally accepted the video call when she'd dropped the phone. A thrill raced through her. *He actually called!* God, she hoped she didn't look like a scarecrow. She raked her fingers through her hair, glad she'd put on a nightshirt before dropping into bed, and tried to sound unconcerned. "Hey, what's up?"

"I need you to retrieve me."

"Agent Randall let you go?" She'd been certain the NSA agent would keep the aliens locked down until Judgment Day.

Zhiruto shook his head. "I'll explain everything once you arrive."

She narrowed her eyes. This sounded like trouble, and the last thing she needed was the NSA breathing down her neck for aiding and abetting an alien fugitive. "Where are you?"

"I have transmitted my coordinates to your vehicle. Please hurry."

He hacked into my police cruiser? She shouldn't be surprised. His alien tech could probably access anything. She supposed it wouldn't hurt to hear him out. He was a fellow law enforcement officer, after all, even if he was from another planet. "All right. I'll be there as soon as I can."

She hung up and swung her legs off the mattress, glancing around her disaster of a bedroom. Her gown lay in a heap on the floor near the bathroom, and several days' worth of dirty laundry overflowed her hamper. A matching basket of unfolded clean clothes rested at the foot of her bed. Although she figured the last place he'd be seeing was her bedroom, she quickly shoved everything into her closet and tidied the top of her dresser before pulling on a fresh set of jeans and a black v-neck tank top.

Pepper followed her into the bathroom, watching with hopeful eyes as Lora applied a coat of mascara to her lashes and blush to her cheeks. "You're staying here, girl." She scratched the coonhound's bony skull. "I'll be back soon."

Huffing in resignation, Pepper lay in the hallway with her chin on her paws.

Lora raced downstairs two steps at a time, passing through the outdated kitchen with its dark pressboard cupboards and mustard-yellow refrigerator that refused to die. The house was tiny and needed major renovations, but she'd gotten it for a song, and it was in a decent neighborhood.

Her police cruiser waited in the driveway outside the back door. The sounds of music and voices echoed from neighboring yards where people had gathered in hope of catching a glimpse of the aliens or their ships. She turned on the car's onboard navigation system, and a map appeared with a pinned location near the dog park only minutes away. She started the engine and backed out of the driveway, pulling into traffic.

Small groups of people dressed like aliens peppered the sidewalks. Bobbing plastic antennae, green makeup, and flashy silver clothing seemed to be the favored style, even though they looked nothing like the aliens at the party, let alone the aliens from the old Beijing photographs. The assassin would have no trouble blending into a crowd like this.

Her phone rang, and she glanced at the dash to see Maise calling. Rather late for her friend to call, but she probably wanted the scoop on Zhiruto. With this latest development, Lora wasn't ready to talk. She declined the call and made the turn onto Maple Street. Every parking space and driveway was crammed with cars, and some lawns had hand-scrawled signs posted with fees to park on the grass. People sat on lawn chairs and picnic tables holding beer bottles and gazing toward the sky.

This is going to get interesting, she thought as she approached Zhiruto's location. She stopped next to a white Toyota Corolla parked at the curb and scanned the nearby houses for a tall blue alien. Porches were full of people, and two houses down there were teenagers playing glow-in-the-dark badminton on the front lawn, but there was no sign of Zhiruto.

Behind her, a green Suburban pulled to a stop. *Great.* Now she was blocking traffic. She didn't want to turn on her lights and draw extra attention, so she rolled down her window and waved for the vehicle to pass. As the SUV pulled slowly by, three kids in the back seat gawked at her.

Just then, the approach of helicopter rotors swelled to a deafening roar. She leaned forward to look through the windshield as a fleet of six military transport choppers passed overhead, heading for the park. *Damn, Agent Randall called in the cavalry.* Were they looking for Zhiruto?

Someone tapped against her passenger side window, and she jerked her head around. Zhiruto's face peered at her through the glass, half-shrouded by a yellow baby blanket covered with pink bunnies. She hit the door lock and he slid into the front seat with graceful ease.

"I suggest we leave the vicinity immediately, Loragriffin."

She shifted the car into drive and pulled onto the street, thinking he looked comically adorable in the blanket. "What's going on? Are those helicopters looking for you?"

"No one will look for me. Agent Randall believes I'm dead."

She glanced at him in surprise. "How'd you pull that off?"

"I merely entered my resting state and he assumed I was dead."

Thinking of the survivor, she conceded that was entirely plausible. She turned the corner toward her house. "Crafty deception."

Within minutes, she pulled into her driveway. She cut the engine and turned to him, wanting to ask more questions, but he was already getting out of the car.

She scrambled after him as he strode up the two steps to her back door. Much as she didn't like taking a strange alien into her home, she liked standing on an open, exposed porch with him even less, so she shoved her key in the lock and opened the door.

Pepper sat waiting in the darkness, tail thumping against the floor like a club. She was making the throaty, excited whine of greeting she used when her favorite people came to visit.

Zhiruto put a hand on the dog's head, which made Pepper wiggle even harder. The fact that Pepper liked him helped ease Lora's wariness about allowing a stranger into her house.

Stepping past Pepper, Zhiruto glanced around the galley-style kitchen. "Is this your domicile?"

She discreetly nudged an empty pizza box on the counter into the trash before turning on a light. Luckily the rest of the kitchen was clean. "Yes, this is my house. Now please tell me what you want from me. I could get in big trouble for sheltering you."

He let the baby blanket slip down around his shoulders, revealing his long mane of navy blue hair, and moved to peer through the archway into the living room. Somehow, he'd acquired a tee shirt, and it hugged his shoulders and arms in a most flattering fashion. Her gaze slid down his backside to admire the rest of him.

He turned back around and she took a heartbeat too long to return her gaze to his, flushing when she realized she'd been caught staring. She crossed her arms to hide her embarrassment. "There's no one else here, so speak freely."

He crossed his arms, as well. "As you suggested, I didn't tell the NSA about the *burendo*. Agent Randall has men searching outside the park, but they believe they're searching for someone who doesn't look human. The assassin will easily escape their notice. I need your assistance finding him."

She thought about the people gathering outside. "Is he a threat to other people?"

"He has no reason to harm the natives unless he's cornered." The *chop-chop-chop* of helicopters flying low overhead rattled the house, and Zhiruto glanced toward the ceiling. "Your NSA doesn't seem capable of being discreet. It's good Agent Randall doesn't know the truth, or the *burendo* would redouble his efforts to fit in."

She laughed out loud. "The NSA prides itself on operating under the radar." Then she recalled the fleet of choppers and another thought occurred to her. "Unless the government's just covering something bigger."

"What do you mean?"

She pictured secret underground test labs with aliens floating in tanks. Not wanting to alarm him about the other aliens still in the park, she said, "Just that it might be good you got away when you did."

Zhiruto moved to examine the photos on her fridge. He pointed to the gap-toothed school photo of her niece. "Do you have children?"

"No. Those are my brother's kids." She set her keys and phone on the counter near the door.

He twisted his head to look at her. "Do human siblings care for one another's progeny?"

"If by care for you mean have affection, then yes. But I'm not a caregiver. They live in Houston, so I only get to see them a couple of times a year."

"Why do you not have children of your own?" His gaze was so intense, she wanted to take a step backward. *Or forward.* She couldn't decide.

She settled on a frown. "Not every woman wants kids, you know."

He smiled slowly, his attention sliding down over her breasts and hips. "You would make beautiful children."

Never in her life had she been turned on by baby-making references, but everything about Zhiruto put her hormones into overdrive. *Maybe I should just fuck him and get it out of my system.* Except Zhiruto was an alien. She had no idea if his species even had sex—they were technically amorphous blobs, after all. Yet his present form was so gorgeous, she couldn't help imagining what he might look like naked.

She forced herself to return her focus to his request for help. "Let's go to the living room and discuss your plan."

Moving past him through the archway, she went straight to the curtains facing the street and yanked them closed. The last thing she needed was a nosy neighbor spotting a hunky blue alien sitting on her sofa.

"Please forgive the dog hair," she said as she clicked on a lamp. She turned to find Zhiruto already sitting on the couch with Pepper next to him, the dog's head planted on his lap. An unbidden smile twisted Lora's lips. "And forgive the pesky dog. Pepper, get down."

He smiled back. "Pepper is quite affectionate. I can see why humans are attracted to these quadrupeds."

She nudged Pepper to the floor, then sat at the opposite end from Zhiruto. The coonhound shoved her head into Lora's lap, tail wagging leisurely. "I'm glad you like her."

Zhiruto adjusted his seating, bringing himself closer to her, and reached over to scratch behind Pepper's ears. "I like both of you."

Good Lord, could he be any cheesier? Yet at the same time, Lora was compelled to like him. He was genuine in a way few human men could manage.

"Thanks. We like you, too." She cleared her throat. "So, about this assassin. Do you have a plan to find him or her?"

"I don't believe the assassin will have ventured far from the park. He will take time to learn your customs before trying to blend in."

"You keep saying he. Are you sure it's a man?"

"The assassin is male. All Kirenai are male."

"All male?" She tried to wrap her head around that thought. "How does that work?"

Pepper pulled away and grabbed her chew toy, laying down nearby. Zhiruto dropped his hand to the cushions between their thighs, just touching the edge of Lora's leg. "As shapeshifters, we're able to breed with females of many species."

Alien breeding should be the last thing on her mind. Yet at that moment, with his hand against her thigh, it was all she could think of. Before she knew it, she was leaning toward him.

8

*D*esire radiated off Loragriffin, filling Zhiruto like a drug. He knew he needed to focus on finding the assassin, but when she tilted her chin, he was unable to resist. He leaned forward, capturing her lips.

That first moment of contact felt like an explosion that rocked him to his core. This was the sensation every Kirenai dreamed of. The instant a perfect match was made. He no longer cared if he impregnated her and lost his job guarding the prince. This was all that mattered. He opened his mouth and pressed his tongue between her lips, needing to taste her as if she was life itself.

She responded with matching passion, opening beneath his questing tongue in a way that made his human heartbeat quicken. She was the most amazing female he'd ever encountered, and he knew once he had her, there'd be no turning back. His Iki'i was drunk with desire. She was intoxicating. Irresistible. Before he even realized what he was doing, his hand was cupping her breast.

She moaned into his mouth with an abandon that made his cock swell and strain against the human clothing he wore.

He leaned closer, devouring her with his kiss, fingers pinching the taut bud of her nipple through her clothing.

She reached for his waistband, unfastening the button. His cock sprang free with a life of its own, surging toward her groping hand with a need that made him dizzy.

A small noise of surprise escaped her, and she broke the kiss, her gaze going to his crotch. "Good Lord, you're huge."

Her trepidation brought him back to his senses. He couldn't take her like he wanted to. Couldn't risk impregnating her. Kirenai fathers had to focus everything on their children, and his duty to the prince had to come first. He attempted to close his fly, but the swollen shaft was in the way. "We must stop."

She put one hand over his, her desire still pounding his Iki'i. "I didn't mean I don't want you."

"I won't risk impregnating you." His attention dropped to her middle. The thought of putting a child in there made his cock grow harder.

A soft laugh brought his attention back to her face. "You won't impregnate me. That's what birth control's for, and I'm a firm believer in doubling up. I'm pretty sure we can get a condom over you."

His universal translator flooded with information about 'birth control' and 'condoms.' Most species in the consortium struggled to keep birth rates up, but humans were so prolific, it made sense they had developed some form of control over impregnation. He relaxed his grip on the closure of his pants. "You will not get pregnant?"

She pushed his hand away and wrapped her fingers around his shaft. "Don't they have contraceptives on your planet?"

He shuddered in pleasure, barely able to think as she stroked upward over his sensitive crown. "We have no need. Children are rare blessings."

"Wait right here." She pushed off the couch and hurried up a set of stairs behind a huge telemonitor mounted on the wall. Within a few moments, she was back with a shiny square gripped in one hand. She tossed it onto the small table beside where they sat.

"This is the condom you spoke of?"

"Yeah, but we don't have to put it on just yet." She straddled him, the heat between her legs teasing his exposed cock through her pants.

Leaning forward, she set her lips once more to his, fingers threading into the back of his hair.

Now that he didn't need to concern himself with children, his desire returned full force. He placed his hands on her hips and let her have her way.

She kissed him deeply, rocking her hips in a slow rhythm against his erection until he was so hard he thought he might break. She made small moans of pleasure, but he could feel her yearning for something more. He moved his hand to the button at her waist, glad he'd experienced the use of human clothing on his own body.

He deftly flicked it open and slid his fingers inside and over the silken hair of her mons. She gasped, back arching and legs widening as she hovered over his lap. He delved deeper, entering the slit between her legs. Her hot wet nub pulsed beneath his fingers. His Iki'i thrumming with her pleasure, he rubbed his middle finger slowly over the swelling bundle of nerves, loving the way her hips flexed to meet the rhythm.

This was the most primal experience he'd ever had, an instinct he'd never known. He followed the slit deeper, finding a well of moisture. Desire to fill that space—to plunge deeply into her—consumed him.

As he thought it, she broke away, standing to wriggle the fabric of her pants down, exposing herself to his gaze.

His cock pulsed from the gap in his pants, the thick shaft seeming to have a desire all its own as it throbbed in response to her naked bottom half.

She dropped to her knees, and her mouth found the tip of his shaft. The sudden hot, wet heat engulfed him with nearly overwhelming pleasure. Her tongue swirled over the head, making him buck upward, seeking more. Her mouth took in half of his length while her other hand circled his base, pumping up and down.

His eyes rolled back in his head. He'd never had a lover so intent on pleasing him.

Her other hand slid inside his pants beneath his cock, and he knew she was looking for his balls. He had to concentrate on making his secondary shaft subside; the mating shaft was for when the time came to bond with a mate and gift her the genetic markers that would brand her as his forever. *This time is for pleasure alone,* he reminded himself.

She found his balls, and he was once again surprised by the level of sensation he felt as she fondled them while she sucked. Her groping was awkward, hindered by the pants he still wore. He wanted to feel more, to have her cup them and roll them, to feel them slap against her ass as he penetrated her over and over.

Done with this nonsensical human clothing, he pushed her gently back and stood, peeling the thick fabric off his legs.

Releasing an appreciative breath, she reached for the condom, tearing the small square open with her teeth. She extracted a thin disk. "Here."

Settling the disk over his crown, she rolled the edges down over his shaft. The material encircled him tightly, but it wasn't the pressure he was craving.

He pulled her to her feet then gripped her hips and lifted her until the heat of her center poised over his shaft. "I wish to penetrate you."

Her eyes were round, the black of her pupils nearly consuming the chocolate brown irises. She drew her legs up around his waist and wrapped her arms around his neck, leaning in to kiss him. Her heels dug into his backside, driving him into her slickness as she angled her hips to accept him.

He eased her over his shaft, adjusting his size to meet her pleasure until their hips made contact. *Kuzara,* she was perfect, her desire matching his own. The condom dulled his sensation slightly, but that might be a good thing, considering her effect on him.

She tilted her hips toward him, grinding and squirming delightfully as her walls stretched to accommodate his girth.

"Oh, God, fuck me," she murmured against his lips before once more plunging her tongue into his mouth.

He thrust forward, pulling her against him, then lifted and plunged again. The building friction was like an approaching storm, tumultuous and wild. His rhythm grew more furious until Loragriffin was moaning in time to his thrusts.

Then her channel pulsed and she shouted, "Yes!"

An orgasm rippled through her, but he kept driving, knowing he could take her higher. He was reveling in both her pleasure and his own, focusing the head of his cock against the spot that sent her into ecstasy. He could feel the tension inside her, the need to come building once more. Over and over a small voice in his mind repeated, *My mate. Mine.*

He backed her against the stairway wall, hands cupping her ass cheeks, and thrust deeply, driving into her again and again until she screamed his name. Her slickness coated the fronts of his thighs, and their ragged breathing mingled as if there wasn't enough air in the room. But he continued pumping forward, filling her with the long thickness of his primary cock.

His mating shaft pressed against her ass, slick with her juices. His Iki'i sensed she liked the added pressure, but he forced the shaft into submission. Claiming her wasn't an option. He'd take his pleasure—give her pleasure—and that was all.

Suddenly, her channel clamped down around him with fierce strength. She threw back her head and screamed, "Zhiruto!"

Her juices ran down his legs, and her heels dug into his ass, pressing his hips to hers. His mating shaft jutted forward. Covered in her slickness, it probed her ass. Entered. She moaned again, entire body trembling as her climax rocked her. Buried in her heat, breathing her delicious scent, he shuddered, helpless under the force of his double ejaculation. The sensation was exquisite, beyond anything he'd ever imagined possible.

He held her pressed against the wall for long moments, letting his heartbeat slow. Her breath tickled his ear, and he softly kissed her shoulder before easing his hips back so she could stand.

Then he realized what he'd done.

The condom had done its job, blocking the life force that might create a child.

But there had been no barrier to the shaft that really mattered. The one that set a bond he could never deny.

Loragriffin was now his mate.

9

*L*ora gasped for breath, stars swimming across her vision. She'd had great sex before, but never an orgasm like that. What must've been Zhiruto's finger in her ass had intensified her climax beyond anything she'd imagined possible.

When she finally regained enough focus to look at him once more, the startled look on his face made her sober. "What is it?" She pushed him away, glad the wall was still at her back when her rubber band legs almost refused to hold her. "Did the condom break?"

He looked down to where his cock still stretched the thin sheath to its maximum capacity, the reservoir at the tip now filled with milky blue fluid. "No."

Shit, then what was the matter? Getting pregnant wasn't her worry; her IUD was her primary birth control, and the condom was just assurance against sexually transmitted disease. *Maybe it was terrible sex for him.*

Blanching at the idea, she snatched up her discarded jeans and hurried to the stairs. "I'm going to clean up." She pointed to another door near the kitchen. "There's a bathroom through there if you need it."

She raced up the stairs, thighs slippery and muscles tired. Before she'd reached the upstairs bathroom, she'd stripped out of her shirt and bra. After a quick rinse in the shower, she pulled on a yellow tee shirt and a fresh pair of jeans. She still wasn't ready to face Zhiruto's disappointment. He'd seemed to be enjoying himself, yet there was no denying that horrified expression on his face at the end. *For all I know, he's married.* The idea made her squeamish.

Looking in the mirror, she wiped the residual smudges of mascara from beneath her eyes that the shower hadn't rinsed away. Her cheeks were flushed, her eyes dilated. Usually, that rumpled, satisfied look was a good thing, but right now it made her self-conscious. How could she face him again when he had obvious regrets?

Then another thought occurred to her—what if he'd slipped away already? Only one other time had an evening been so awful that a guy had left without saying goodbye. He'd been an ass to both her and

Pepper, and frankly she'd been relieved when he left. Now, all she could think about was making Zhiruto stay.

The toilet flushed downstairs, and she let out a relieved breath. He was still here. *Maybe I can make things better.*

She winced and turned away from the mirror. That inner voice sounded too much like her mother, who'd always had a man around to "protect" her. Lora had chosen to become a police officer because she refused to let fear rule her life.

Picking up the shirt and bra she'd dropped on her way to the shower, she shoved them into the hamper and muttered, "If he didn't like it, that isn't your fault."

"What isn't your fault?" Zhiruto's voice behind her made her jump.

Lora spun, gaze latching onto Zhiruto standing in the doorway. "God, don't sneak up on me like that."

Pepper hopped onto the bed, lying down with a huff.

"My apologies. I didn't mean to startle you." Zhiruto clamped and unclamped his fists at his sides. He'd refastened his jeans, but was once again shirtless like he'd been at the party. He still looked unhappy. "We must talk, Loragriffin."

She flicked a hand in the air dismissively. "Let's keep it in our pants from now on and focus on the investigation. I have an idea. Let's go downstairs to talk."

Shouldering past him, she exited the room. He tried to grasp her hand, but she evaded him and headed back down the stairs two at a time, trying to put some distance between them. At the bottom, she glanced back to see Zhiruto standing at the top looking down at her. Keeping her voice light, she said, "I imagine it's been a while since you've eaten. Are you hungry?"

"I must admit, yes."

Good. Food would help them both feel better. She headed to the kitchen to get her phone where she'd left it on the counter. Maise had called again, but hadn't left a message. *Boy will I have a story for her once this is all over.* Lora dialed a fried chicken joint that delivered all night, turning around to lean on the counter as Zhiruto followed her into the kitchen. The light from the living room backlit his broad shoulders and narrow hips, and a streetlight outside the kitchen window cut shadows across his face.

"Do you like breasts or thighs?" she asked.

His attention slid from her face to caress her chest and hips. "Both."

From any other man, she would've rolled her eyes at the cheesy pickup line. But when Zhiruto said it, electricity seemed to spark from her nipples to her clit.

Good Lord, how did he continually make her feel like a horny teenager? She was still considering how to respond when the restaurant answered her call.

Swallowing, she looked at the menu flyer stuck to the fridge next to the photos and drawings from her nieces. She knew the menu by heart, but it gave her something to look at besides Zhiruto. She ordered a full bucket of fried chicken plus sides of mashed potatoes and gravy, biscuits, and coleslaw. Then she added a couple of fresh-baked chocolate chip cookies; she didn't usually let herself have dessert but felt like she needed it tonight.

Hanging up, she set the phone aside on the counter. "They usually take about twenty minutes. Want something to drink?"

"Do you have more of that bubbly drink from the auction?"

She raised one eyebrow. "Champagne's not on my budget." Yanking open the fridge, she pulled out two beers, twisted the tops off, and handed one to him. "Try this."

He sipped his hesitantly then tipped the bottle back and drank it all. Damn, the guy must be thirsty. *Or he needs to take the edge off.*

She took several long swallows of her own. Maybe taking the edge off wasn't a bad idea. It felt as if the conflicting voices inside her head were engaged in a fistfight. *I need to do something to make things better.* Stop worrying about him. *But what if it's my fault?* It's not your job to make him feel good. *He tried to stop me and I kept pushing.* He backed you against the wall, not the other way around…

"I sense you're conflicted, Loragriffin."

The way he continually mashed her name together made her get all tingly inside, which only added to her conflict. She shrugged and looked toward Pepper sitting near the back door. Letting the dog out, she watched while Pepper trotted toward the lawn to do her business. "I'm worried about the assassin, that's all."

Zhiruto's warm presence heated her back, hovering just out of range of full contact. "Loragriffin, I've done something unforgivable."

Realizing an alien now stood in full view of her neighbors, she pivoted and put a hand on his chest to push him backward. "Jesus, don't stand where people can see you."

He didn't budge for a second as his hand slid up to cover hers. Then he stepped back into the shadows. The slow glide of his palm skimming the back of her knuckles was almost as erotic as his caress against her breast earlier.

She cleared her throat, trying to keep her head on straight. "What have you done?"

"You are my mate."

Stunned silence filled the kitchen as she blinked at him, trying to understand. *Holy shit, does he think we're married now just because we had sex?* Dread settled into her bones. "No I'm not."

Pepper padded back inside, and Lora closed the door with a hard thud.

Zhiruto continued to stare at her, his dark eyes glittering in the dim light. "We are bonded."

"Don't worry about it, really. It was just sex," she lied. Hell if she was going to admit it had been the best sex of her life, though she was also relieved to learn he hadn't hated the encounter like she'd first worried.

Downing the rest of her beer, she set the bottle on the counter and marched into the living room, careful not to brush against him as she passed. She flopped onto the couch next to Pepper, letting the dog remain on the cushions as a barrier to Zhiruto if he took the seat next to her. The coonhound put her head on Lora's lap, eyes rolling to look at Zhiruto as he followed them into the room.

The big blue alien remained standing. "I sense you're angry."

"I'm not angry. You're just confused. And you're on Earth now, so we have different rules." She knew she was being a bitch, but she couldn't help it. She didn't need a permanent man, didn't want one, and she wasn't about to buy into some alien code of honor about having sex. And as nice as it might be to have a hot, nearly seven-foot-tall, blue alien at her beck and call, she didn't want him to stick around because he was required to. He needed to back off.

A low hum that was almost too soft to hear reached her and Zhiruto's mouth tightened. He lifted his forearm. As before, a screen materialized above it, and the blue face of the alien she'd seen with Georgie appeared.

He and Zhiruto exchanged a few words in a language Lora didn't understand, then Zhiruto angled the screen to include Lora. "This human is a member of local law enforcement," he said in English. "She's helping me track the assassin."

Georgie's face appeared on the screen. "Lora?"

Lora shot to her feet, moving closer. Georgie's face glowed with multicolored lights that created a pattern over her skin, extending well below where Lora could see on the screen. "Georgie, where are you? What's going on with your skin?"

"Oh." Georgie lifted a glowing arm to admire it, an amazed smile twisting her mouth. "It's painted on, don't worry. I'm fine." She looked back up to meet Lora's eyes. "What's happening there? Is everyone okay?"

"Depends on your definition of okay. No humans seem to have been harmed, but there are a ton of dead aliens laying around." She explained everything that had happened except the sexual debacle. She wasn't ready to talk about it, especially with Zhiruto looking over her shoulder. Before Georgie could ask any leading questions, Lora asked, "Where are you?"

"I'm currently orbiting an alien planet, believe it or not." Georgie laughed, sounding surprisingly relaxed about it. "I'm heading back to Earth now. I should arrive in a few days."

"Girl, don't." Lora held up a palm, worry for her friend rising in her chest. "The NSA's looking for you. They consider you a person of interest, and they're assholes. You do not want to end up in their hands."

Georgie chewed her lip and glanced at the blue alien lingering beside her. "I guess I can stay here a while. But I'll be in touch. Take care of yourself, okay?"

"You, too." Lora blew her a kiss, and Zhiruto turned the screen back on himself, pacing away to speak a few more words.

The doorbell rang, making Lora jump. Pepper responded in kind, lurching off the sofa with a baying bark as she moved to the door. All this alien intrigue was making her twitchy, and she didn't like it. She wasn't timid or weak. She was a woman who took the bull by the balls. Still, she peered through the peephole to be certain it was the food delivery before she opened the door.

She carried the food to the kitchen and tore open the bags, inhaling the savory warm scent of fried chicken. The familiar scent was comforting, grounding. *Normal.* And it helped her understand what she had to do.

As soon as they finished eating, she was going to find the assassin and put both aliens on a spaceship back home.

10

Zhiruto was relieved the prince was safe, but the call had reminded him of his duty. First, he'd missed the transport window and was unable to escort his prince home. Now he'd been dallying with Loragriffin while the *burendo* was fortifying his disguise. Every second increased the assassin's ability to blend in with the natives.

At least his mate wanted to stay focused on the hunt. *Another reason she's my perfect match.* But talk about mate bonds could wait. He followed the smell of unfamiliar spices and oil into the kitchen where Loragriffin was assembling two platters.

She spoke without looking up. "So, my idea about finding the assassin sort of depends on you. If he's outside the park, do you think he'll still be shielding himself from your icky-whatever sense?"

"Iki'i," he pronounced. "Since there are not Kirenai searching for him outside the park, there would be no reason to expend the energy, so I think not."

She thrust a full plate toward him. "Good." Picking up a large golden brown piece of food from her plate, she sank her teeth into it. He found himself mesmerized by the way she licked crumbs off her lips before chewing.

"Fried chicken." She gestured toward the plate in his hands. "Try it."

He looked down. There was a glob of white matter dripping with brown sauce, a small cup of something pale green flecked with orange, a circular item that resembled an unglazed *kazhitu* bun, and a golden brown item with a bone sticking from one end. His translator had identified 'chicken' as one of Earth's animals, so he selected the item with the bone and mimicked the way she'd taken a bite.

His teeth crunched down on salt and grease, then savory juices flooded his mouth. He chewed a few times and swallowed.

"Like it?" she asked.

"Very much."

"Good. There's more in the bucket if you want." She stuck a white plastic fork onto his plate and breezed by him into the living room. "Let's talk in here."

He followed, still munching on the chicken as she flopped onto the sofa and curled her legs up to one side. She'd changed into a new yellow shirt with sleeves that fell halfway to her elbows, the neckline hugging her collarbone. On the front was a swooped blue slash. He'd liked her better in the sleeveless tunic that exposed her skin, but the yellow of this one suited her rich auburn hair. She'd pulled it together at the back of her head, and he longed to let it down and run his fingers through its silky tresses. To strip her clothing from her and explore her body more thoroughly than he'd done during their previously rushed coupling.

Keep your distance, he told himself. Now that he'd shared the mate bond with her, all it would take was one playful glance from her and he'd want to pounce. He moved to a wooden rocking chair next to the window.

From where Loragriffin sat on the sofa, a flush of disappointment washed his way. He forced himself to ignore it. There would be time to lavish her with attention later, once they'd wrapped up this case.

Pepper skulked to the far edge of the sofa and lay down on the floor with her muzzle resting on her paws. He could sense both craving and resignation coming from the dog, but Loragriffin made no move to share her food with the animal.

"Tell me more of your plan, Loragriffin." He tore off another bite of chicken.

"First, we need to make you look a bit more human so I can get you into the precinct. It shouldn't be too hard—we have boatloads of people walking around town dressed as aliens, so all we have to do is make you look like someone wearing a bad costume."

He frowned. "Should we not try our utmost to disguise me well?"

"Most of the costumes are nothing more than plastic antennae and green face paint. Looking too perfect will draw attention." She stirred the fluffy white mound on her plate and then took a bite.

"Then I will defer to your judgment." If she thought a silly costume was all that was needed to mingle undetected among humans, then he had to believe her. But it meant the assassin would find it easier to hide, as well. He was beginning to lose hope of picking up a trail.

He focused on his plate. He'd always enjoyed sampling strange dishes during his travels with the prince—probably why the assassin had thought poisoning the food was a good plan. He hesitated a brief moment as he thought of the auction, then shrugged his concern aside. Loragriffin would never try to kill him.

Stirring the white mash as Loragriffin had done, he took a bite. The bland flavor was not to his liking, but he swallowed politely before picking up the thing that looked like a *kazhitu* bun. It had been split in two, and the center had been lavished with a rich yellow oil. He took a bite. "This is delicious. What do you call it?"

"That's a buttermilk biscuit. The white stuff is mashed potatoes, though I'm pretty sure they use instant, not the real thing. The little bowl is coleslaw."

He finished the other half of the biscuit in one bite, nodding at her in appreciation. She laughed. The sound sent a thrill of pleasure through him. He liked it when she laughed. He needed to discover more ways to make her happy.

"There's more of everything on the counter, and I have cookies for dessert when you're ready. Eat up." She stood, taking her plate toward the kitchen. "My brother left some boxes in my shed, and I think his clothes will fit you. Be right back."

The moment she was gone, Pepper rose and moved closer to sit in front of him, the animal's earlier resignation replaced by hope. He'd seen some of the females at the auction sharing food off their plate. Perhaps one was not supposed to offer until the quadruped asked? Scooping up a forkful of mashed potatoes, he held it out to her. "Would you like some?"

The dog leaned forward and swept out her tongue, licking the fork clean. An overwhelming sense of appreciation and delight filled Zhiruto's senses.

Zhiruto smiled. "I can see why the humans enjoy your species' company."

He sampled a bite of the green and orange flecked coleslaw. The slightly sour flavor reminded him of the *ayabe* his father used to make, and he finished it with gusto in between sharing bites of the potatoes with Pepper. By the time Loragriffin returned, her arms draped with clothing, he and Pepper had cleaned off his plate and helped themselves to seconds.

Loragriffin took one look at the dog's head in his lap and sighed. "Pepper, no begging."

The dog flinched and slunk back to the end of the sofa with her tail down.

Worried he'd offended, Zhiruto said, "My apologies. I saw other females at the party feeding their dogs, and Pepper seemed hungry."

A smile tugged the corners of Loragriffin's mouth. "She's a big fat liar, but it's okay. Just please don't give her any bones. And try not to make a habit of it."

"As you wish." He nodded and stood, setting his plate aside and eyeing the various colored fabric in her arms. "This clothing belonged to your brother?"

"Yeah. He stayed with me awhile when he and his wife were on the outs."

He liked the affection she radiated when speaking about her brother. "I've always wondered what it would be like to have siblings."

She tossed the clothes on the sofa and picked up a burgundy shirt. "You're an only child?"

"Most Kirenai are. Only rarely do bonded couples produce more than one offspring, and family units remain close throughout their lives. What about your parents? Do they live nearby?"

She shrugged. "My dad's not really in the picture. Never was. My mom lives with her current boyfriend in Tampa."

He'd been informed that humans made excellent mothers and had thereby assumed they and their offspring remained close for life, but Loragriffin's emotions when it came to her mother were more tolerant than affectionate. "I'm sorry you're not close."

"I'm as close as I'd like to be." She gave him a tight smile and held out the shirt. "I hope it doesn't smell too musty. Try this on."

He took the shirt she offered and pulled it over his head. Loragriffin liked his large muscles, and he'd purposefully exaggerated them for her benefit, but now they were making squeezing into the new clothing difficult. Concentrating on his matrix, he tried to condense himself to a smaller size and discovered he couldn't. The shirt was now twisted awkwardly around his shoulders, and he glanced with embarrassment toward her. She liked it when he was graceful, and at the moment, he was anything but.

But instead of disappointment, he was met with a rush of arousal.

Only then did he realize why he couldn't shift; when a Kirenai found a mate, his form was set, permanently held in the form his mate preferred. He was bonded to Loragriffin, which meant he was now and forever tied to this human shape.

Which also meant he could no longer serve as the prince's personal guard. His duties relied upon him being able to alter his appearance, to remain incognito along with the prince. His stomach roiled as if he was on a ship that had just lost gravity. If he could no longer adjust himself, he would have to resign. Who was he if he wasn't the prince's personal guard?

He tugged at the stretchy shirt, rolling his shoulders to make it fit. There wasn't time to wallow. Not now, when he was technically still on the job—the last job of his career. If he could now only look human, he planned to make the most of it.

He was going to locate the assassin at all costs.

11

*L*ora watched Zhiruto pull her brother's old long-sleeved tee shirt over his head and tried not to drool over his flexing muscles. He stretched the shirt to maximum capacity, and she halfway wished she'd brought in a change of pants, too, just for a chance to get to see him step out of the old ones.

Stop it, she scolded herself. The guy was crazy enough with his talk of being her mate. She shouldn't encourage him.

Except she wanted to. They worked well together. The sex was amazing. Even Pepper adored him. Would it be so bad to make Zhiruto a permanent fixture in her life?

He finally got the fabric settled snugly over his torso and adjusted the tight arms across his biceps. She'd selected a plain shirt with no logo so as not to encourage anyone to read it when they ventured outside. But people were still going to look—his biceps were droolworthy, even beneath the cloth, and the deep burgundy color looked fantastic against his blue skin.

"That will do," she said, forcing her gaze away. "Let me grab some makeup. We'll need to cover some of that blue."

She hurried up the stairs and rummaged through her makeup drawer to find a tube of concealer. Gathering foundation, liquid blush, and several shades of lipstick, she stuffed them into a travel bag. Then she took a moment to check her own face, adjusting her ponytail and dusting her cheeks with some blush. *I'm not doing it for him. I'm doing it because we're going out soon.*

But she knew it was a lie.

She'd always told herself she was fine without a man, without the baggage of caring what someone thought or did. Yet deep inside, she wanted to please Zhiruto.

Returning to the living room, she discovered him lying on his back on the floor with his knees up. Pepper lay half-sprawled across his chest, nuzzling his jaw, tail wagging with pure affection. Lora's heart threatened to melt right out of her body. A man with a dog was sexy enough, but a man loving on *her* dog was downright irresistible, just like when she'd walked in and found him feeding Pepper off his fork.

Unable to restrain her smile, she bypassed them and went to the kitchen, bringing a chair back and setting it near the lamp. "I'm going to need you to sit here."

He pushed Pepper off his chest and rose, moving with a grace that made Lora's insides flutter. Pepper rolled playfully on her back, trying to entice him to return, then gave up and focused on her chew toy as Zhiruto relaxed into the chair.

She unscrewed the cap to her foundation. "Let's see if I can make you more human."

"I'm already human for you, Loragriffin."

She didn't know why, but the statement made her heart stutter. "Stop the flirting and hold still."

His hair was mussed from lying on the floor, and she ran her fingers through it to get it off his forehead, trying not to let her hand tremble at the familiarity of the gesture. Being around him felt strangely *right*. A weird mix of comfortable and uncomfortable at the same time. If she had to define the feeling, she might call herself giddy, not that she'd ever admit it.

She bit her lip as she dotted the applicator along his forehead at his hairline. The peachy shade was a complete opposite to his vibrant blue skin tone, and she had to put it on extra thick. If she made just a line around his face, it would look like his blue tone was makeup, and not the other way around. Using the tip of one finger, she blended it back toward his hair. His masculine smell pervaded her senses, and touching the warm, smooth skin of his forehead put her hormones in gear again. She smoothed the concealer toward his temple, breathing shallowly as she worked, though all she could think about was how close he was.

His eyes were closed, his face tilted slightly toward her, and his hands lay relaxed on his thighs. How could he look so damned comfortable when she was all fluttery inside? It wasn't fair.

She examined his slightly parted lips. Vivid blue, yet utterly kissable, surrounded by the perfect amount of scruff. Her own mouth tingled at the memory of that stubble against her face and neck, the way his kisses had felt. She wanted to feel his mouth on hers again, to experience his whiskers in unmentionable places, to smell herself on him as his arms embraced her…

His dark eyes popped open, full of a sudden hunger that took her breath away. *Stop being a silly schoolgirl. We decided to keep it above the belt.* But her imagination was all over the place when it came to this guy—especially the naughty places. Throat tight, she said, "We need to do something with your lips. They're too blue."

Stepping away from him, she pawed through her small bag of cosmetics, opening and closing several tubes of lipstick before settling on a rosy shade she thought might look natural. Trying to stay no-nonsense, she clipped, "Open up."

Still relaxed against the chair back and regarding her from beneath hooded lids, Zhiruto smiled and widened his knees.

Damn. That pushed every button she had. Her gaze fell to the bulge at the front of his pants—probably exactly what he wanted. *Or what I wanted.* She dragged her attention back up to meet his eyes. "I meant your mouth."

"I can do that, too." His voice had a low growl that seemed to connect straight to her pussy. He parted his lips.

She cleared her throat. Maybe she should leave his lips alone. Who'd really be looking at his mouth, anyway? But it would be foolish to go to all this effort and let her plan fail because she'd been a coward about one final detail.

Holding the lipstick out like a talisman, she stepped closer, feeling as if she was entering a trap as she stepped between his massive thighs. His eyes stayed locked on hers as she swiped the lipstick over his lower lip, then his upper. The way his flesh gave subtly under the pressure felt so erotic. She longed to smudge the lipstick with her fingers like she'd done the concealer. She could imagine his teeth gently catching her finger, his heated mouth sucking it gently…

She gulped, clutching the tube of lipstick tighter to keep herself in check. "Press them together."

His knees closed against her thighs. The heat of his breath penetrated the thin fabric of her tee shirt right over her breasts.

"I meant your lips," she choked out, realizing she'd put her free hand on his shoulder for balance.

He brought one hand up and wrapped long fingers around her forearm, turning his head slightly and running his nose down the inside of her wrist. "You smell amazing."

A shiver coursed through her. "Stop," she rasped. "We're on duty."

"You're right." He gently bit the base of her palm below her thumb, sending rockets of desire straight to her heart. "Let's get on with it." He released her arm and put his hands on her waist, pushing her back a step as he rose.

For a flash, she thought he'd said, "get it on." She could barely breathe, only let her head fall back to look up at his impressive height, her breasts barely brushing his chest. *What is wrong with me?* It felt like she was under a spell, dumbfounded and paralyzed. "Are you using some alien voodoo trick on me?"

"Voodoo trick? I don't understand." He frowned at her. "Do you feel unwell?"

"No, I'm just… not thinking straight. It's strange." She managed to take a step away from him and pick up a pair of aviator sunglasses and a pair of plastic devil horns she'd found in the shed. "Put these on and we're good to go."

He complied, looking like a cross between 007 and an extra in a low budget sci-fi movie. "You haven't told me the rest of your plan," he said, adjusting the elastic holding the horns to his head. "Why must we go to your precinct?"

"We need to use my desk computer to access the secure dispatch logs. The one in my car won't let me. Your assassin may be able to look human, but he's bound to do something strange or even illegal and get reported. I bet with a little elbow grease, we can pick up a trail."

Zhiruto chuckled. "Your elbows are not greasy, but even so, we don't need to go to your precinct to view the logs." He brought up his arm and opened the floating screen. "I can access it from here."

Of course he could. He'd hacked her car's navigation system earlier.

An interface just like the precinct computer screen floated in the air. He shifted closer and angled his arm to allow her to view it. "Are these the files you require?"

She pointed at a dropdown. "Go there."

After directing him through several steps, they located the logs. Within a few minutes, he'd run them through some sort of program that weeded out most of the irrelevant reports.

"How do you know they're not relevant?" she asked.

"We've been watching humans for a long time. There are certain tells." He opened the first file. "These are the incidents that potentially included our assassin. Good thinking, by the way."

She hated to admit it, but she beamed under his praise. "Let me see them."

The first file was a masked robbery. She doubted the assassin would bother to rob a convenience store, let alone wear a mask while doing it. Next up was a familiar address—Yappy Hour Dog Kennels and Grooming.

"Maise?" she gasped. "That's my friend's place."

"The female who took care of Pepper at the auction?"

"Yeah." She quickly read the log; the owner had called in to report a trespasser, but when officers arrived she brushed it off as a mistake. Guilt ran through Lora as she recalled the missed calls from her friend. "Something's not right. I need to call her." She rushed to the kitchen where she'd left her phone and dialed Maise. The call went to voicemail.

Zhiruto followed her. "We must go there immediately."

"I shouldn't have ignored her calls." She snatched her keys from the counter and stuffed her phone in her back pocket. "What if she's in trouble?" Yanking open the back door, she froze.

Agent Randall stood on her porch backed by two armed guards.

Zhiruto didn't understand why Loragriffin stood frozen in the doorway until she raised her hands and said, "Put away your weapons. No one here's a threat."

Striding closer, he saw Agent Randall outside, flanked by two men holding guns.

Pepper skulked up beside him and growled. She was feeling almost as protective as he was, and he put a hand on her head to communicate his shared purpose.

"Pepper, get back," Loragriffin commanded.

The animal obeyed but continued to growl.

"Get in the car." Agent Randall stepped backward off the porch and indicated a wheeled black vehicle parked behind Loragriffin's smaller car. "Both of you."

"We've done nothing wrong." She crossed her arms, belligerence thudding against his Iki'i.

"Incorrect." Agent Randall pointed toward Zhiruto. "You're harboring an illegal alien—literally. Now move."

Zhiruto put a hand on her shoulder. He didn't like the malice he felt from the three agents outside and wanted to put himself between her and the weapons. But Lora didn't budge from the doorway. His brave mate was trying to protect him.

But now wasn't the time for sentimental pride. He met Agent Randall's eye over her shoulder. "I'll comply if you leave Loragriffin behind."

"Afraid not," said Agent Randall. "She's in too deep to just walk away. Come with me before things escalate any further."

Loragriffin looked over her shoulder at Pepper. "Pepper, you stay." Then she stepped down the porch steps and strode past the agents. "This is going into my report."

Zhiruto loved how confident she was, but he was also frustrated she wasn't giving him a chance to defend her. He followed her cautiously down the porch steps. The oily sensation of Randall's satisfaction oozed over Zhiruto as he passed by.

"You're in front, *officer.*" Agent Randall opened the passenger side door, emphasizing her title with zero respect.

She glared at him but got into the passenger seat without complaint.

Agent Randall slammed her door then yanked open the one behind it and indicated Zhiruto should get in.

Grinding his teeth, Zhiruto ducked inside. Randall nudged him to scoot over next to another agent before climbing in beside him, keeping his gun pointed at Loragriffin's back through the seat. "Everyone behave, now."

The other agent in the back seat held his weapon wedged against Zhiruto's side.

Zhiruto kept his voice calm and said, "Your concerns are with me, not the female. Let her go."

The third agent settled into the driver's seat and started the vehicle.

Agent Randal smirked as they backed down the driveway. "You're a long way from home and in no position to dictate terms. Do as we say and she won't get hurt."

"If you harm her, you will pay with your life," Zhiruto growled, hands balled into fists.

Loragriffin twisted around to look at them, but Agent Randall tapped the seat. "Eyes front."

She let out a frustrated breath and turned forward. "Listen, I think I know where the assassin is. We need to get there ASAP."

"You don't need to worry about the assassin anymore," said Randall. "He's back in orbit where he belongs."

Zhiruto clenched his teeth. He should've sensed there was something off when this man refused to cooperate with the investigation. "You let him go?"

Agent Randall sneered. "We received excellent compensation for not interfering."

Loragriffin twisted around again, eyes wide. "Were you part of the assassination plan all along? How could you just let all those people die?"

"Not people. Aliens," Agent Randall spat. "And I do what's necessary for my country and my species. The galactic confederation has continually denied us the means to defend ourselves, so I found a way to get what we need." His glittering eyes focused on Zhiruto. "And you're going to net us even more. The prince's personal bodyguard will be worth a lot to my contacts."

"Who are your contacts?" Zhiruto asked with artificial calm. He couldn't fight back at the moment, but he would find a way out of this. Any information he could gather would be useful.

Agent Randall made a clicking noise with his tongue. "Another instance of you aliens assuming humans are stupid. I'm not going to monologue about all my deepest secrets then let you escape. And you're not as clever as you think. Pretending to die was such a cliché. Your assassin escaped notice by doing the same thing."

Zhiruto groaned inwardly as the pieces came together. The poisoned Kirenai's lack of pain, the worry the poison could be transferred through touch, the false lead about a *burendo* that probably didn't even exist. "The survivor was faking illness."

Agent Randall grinned. "So much for advanced alien technology."

Zhiruto was getting really tired of the man's condescending smirk.

They whizzed past the gate to the park, and a feeling of alarm shot toward him from the front seat. "That was the park," Loragriffin said. "Where are you taking us?"

A flash of uncertainty rose in Agent Randall before slipping beneath the smug surface once more. "Let's just say it's a good thing you like aliens, because I understand you'll be getting familiar with a lot more of them."

"What the hell is that supposed to mean?" she asked.

Zhiruto balled his fists against his thighs. He knew what it meant. Why had it not occurred to him that humans might be feeding their own people to the slavers? "You do realize that the contacts you're working with are some of the most wanted criminals in the galaxy, don't you?"

Agent Randall remained stiff in his seat. "You call them criminals, but they consider themselves freedom fighters. And they're willing to help Earth compete in the galactic hierarchy. A handful of our women is a small price to pay."

"Oh, my God," whispered Loragriffin, once more turning to look at Randall.

The man was vile, more so than Zhiruto could've imagined. He let out a slow breath, never breaking eye contact. "Do your leaders know you've been selling your own females on the black market?"

The other two men had remained surprisingly unemotional this entire time, but Zhiruto didn't have time to probe for deeper feelings. Agent Randall slid his gun between the window and the headrest, pressing the muzzle to the back of her neck. "I said eyes front."

Loragriffin grudgingly turned around to face the oncoming streetlights. "You're a fucking monster."

"Call me what you will, but I'm doing it for the good of humanity. Just like you soon will be. We usually select women who won't be missed, but I'm sure we can find a way to link your disappearance to the assassination. Hell, maybe I'll have you take the fall for it."

"Nobody will believe you." A frantic worry filled the vehicle as Loragriffin processed Agent Randall's words.

It was all Zhiruto could do to keep from strangling the man. Loragriffin could not be handed over to slavers. She was his mate. Like a blow from a sunda lizard's tail, an idea came to him. There was a way to convince Randall to let her go. "Loragriffin will be worthless to slavers."

Agent Randall narrowed his eyes. "What are you talking about?"

"Slavers want human females as breeders. I've claimed Loragriffin as my mate. They will offer you nothing for her when they learn of it."

Randall barked out laughter as the vehicle merged onto a wide street packed with other vehicles moving at a fast pace. "Nice try, alien."

Confusion now mixed with Loragriffin's worry.

Zhiruto continued, wishing he'd been able to have this conversation with his mate in private. "She's already been given the genetic markers that make her unable to bear children for anyone but me. Your buyers will detect this the moment they scan her."

Agent Randall sneered. "Not every alien wants to breed; she's attractive enough to make someone a nice plaything. Hell, they can send her to work in the mines for all I care, as long as they pay me."

"You're pure evil." Loragriffin shook her head, her voice trembling with a mixture of terror and fury.

"Don't judge me. The slave trade was happening long before I got involved. I just found a way to take advantage of the situation. If the emperor would give us the weapons we need instead of closing our planet to trade, we wouldn't have to do it this way. We'd be able to defend ourselves. But he denied our entrance into the confederation, and the only contact we have is with the black market, whether we want it or not. At least this way we get something out of the deal." Agent Randall sat up straighter in his seat. "The women we hand over serve humanity, and the technology they're earning us means soon we'll no longer be at the mercy of the slave traders. We'll stand up for ourselves and join the confederation of planets as we're meant to do."

"You don't really think slavers are going to provide you with technology that can defeat them?" Zhiruto asked. "They want to maintain their trade here, and the last thing they're going to do is arm the natives."

"They think they give us nothing but baubles. Harmless toys and trinkets to numb our minds and soothe our pain. But humans are great at thinking outside the box, and our nation's best scientists have already innovated what they've learned and created weapons that outpace our rivals here on Earth. Eventually, we'll develop weapons that will rival that of any species in the galaxy."

Zhiruto laughed harshly. "You're deluding yourself, Agent Randall. The members of the Senburu who are supplying you are delighted to see you humans squabbling among yourselves. Your inability to get along with one another on your own planet is what keeps humans out of the confederation."

"We'll see about that," said Randall. The vehicle turned down a ramp, leaving traffic behind.

Loragriffin said, "It's not too late to do the right thing, you know. Let's talk about this."

"Shut up, or I'll have you gagged and put in the trunk."

They passed through a small town where all the windows were dark, and soon they turned onto a narrow road lined with overarching trees. The sharp beams of the headlights cut through the darkness, giving them glimpses of small fluttering insects mere moments before pulverizing them.

The driver turned sharply and bumped down a rutted path between the trees. He pulled to a stop in a small clearing.

"Get out." Agent Randall opened his door and climbed out, yanking open Loragriffin's door.

The other agent kept his weapon aimed at Zhiruto. The driver also got out, keeping watch over all of them from the other side of the car while shining a big Maglite toward them.

"That way." Agent Randall jabbed the nose of his gun into Loragriffin's back and herded her down a narrow path between the trees.

Zhiruto's guard said, "Follow them."

The threats were too spread out for Zhiruto to act without risking Loragriffin's life. He stepped onto the uneven trail. This was his first visit to Earth, and the night air smelled cool with a hint of something sour, like rotting vegetation. He wished he was more familiar with what that might mean as they followed the terrain between large, rough-barked trunks.

The two agents at his back maintained a respectable distance, but he could feel their unwavering presence against his Iki'i. He had to do something... and soon. Once they rendezvoused with the slave ship, the traders would have weapons far more deadly than the projectile throwers the humans held.

Although every fiber of his being wanted to resist the idea, a plan began to take shape. He was the one the Senburu wanted, not her. If he resisted or started a fight, it might give her just the break she needed to get away. But he needed to target Agent Randall for this to work.

Picking up his pace, he hurried to catch up.

13

The trail ahead was barely visible in the flashlight beam from several yards behind them, and Lora tried not to trip over the many roots. Every time she thought things had gotten as weird as they possibly could, the universe threw her into a new tailspin. The maniac with a gun at her back was planning to sell her off as some sort of alien sex slave. And what was this mate thing Zhiruto was talking about? No children except with him had to be a lie to try to protect her.

She put a hand against the trunk of a nearby tree to steady herself as she stepped over a root. At least the agents were cocky enough that they hadn't bothered to tie her hands. She was biding her time for an opportunity to disarm Agent Randall, but it would have to be just right or one of the other men would surely shoot her or Zhiruto.

A shout behind her made her spin in time to see Zhiruto tackle Agent Randall from behind. The agent remained obstinately sure-footed as Zhiruto drove him sideways into the tree, grappling for the gun.

Zhiruto's eyes met hers. "Run."

Agent Randall yanked the muzzle down and fired, the shot deafening at close range. Something warm splattered Lora's arm, and pain pinched her side. *Am I shot?* She dropped to a crouch as the men continued to struggle.

Pressing a hand to her waist, it came away sticky, yet she was in surprisingly little pain. *It must just be a flesh wound.* Watching the other agents to make sure they weren't paying any attention to her, she crept around the wide tree trunk into the underbrush.

Another shot rang out, but she couldn't tell from where. One of the agents said, "Get in there. I'll cover you."

Her heart thundered in her ears, and her hands and feet tingled with the need to move. To fight. Her side was beginning to throb, but she pushed the pain aside. She had to act fast if she was going to save Zhiruto. Glancing around the trunk again, she saw one agent edging forward, his attention trained on the men now tussling in front of him. The flashlight lay on the ground behind the third agent, turning the men into silhouettes with their weapons focused on the grapplers.

Her best bet would be to take out the man providing cover, so she tiptoed through the underbrush beside the trail, keeping one hand pressed to the growing stitch in her side. She hoped to spot a branch or rock she could use as a weapon, but what little she could make out on the dark ground showed only a thick layer of leaves.

She came out on the trail behind the man in the rear and paused. If she tried to sneak up on him, he'd likely turn the gun on her, which would only end badly. But if she swept in fast enough, she might be able to take him down with the first blow. She'd done plenty of mat tumbling in her kickboxing lessons, but she wasn't sure she could take him down with her fists alone, and her wound was making her feel woozy.

Her gaze dropped to the flashlight. It would make a decent club if she could reach it.

Taking a few quick breaths, she darted forward, doing a tuck and roll to grab the mag-lite. Her fingers wrapped around the long handle, and she rocked back to her feet, gritting her teeth as she swung a wide arc toward the man's head.

A resounding thud filled the air as the metal shaft made contact. He dropped like a stone, his pistol cartwheeling into the leafy underbrush.

The other agent rounded on her, the muzzle of his pistol seeking a target. Dropping the flashlight, she dove into the darkness beside the trail. A deafening shot split the forest, close enough behind for her to feel the rush of displaced air. Barely daring to breathe, she belly-crawled through the brush toward the men.

The agent shouted, "Damn bitch came in behind us. Richmond's down."

Zhiruto yelled, "Loragriffin, run!"

No way was she going to leave Zhiruto here to face them alone. After all they'd been through, he was her partner, and she refused to leave him behind. Through the trees she could see the agent half-lit by the reflected glow from the flashlight and panning his gun along the treeline where she lay hiding. She halted her crawl, hand pressed to the growing wetness on her side. She should check it and staunch the bleeding, but there wasn't time.

Agent Randall gasped, "Ignore her and get this fucking alien off me."

Reluctantly, the agent turned toward where Zhiruto had Randall pinned, one knee on his chest, the other on a wrist while he grappled with the gun in Randall's free hand.

The agent who was still on his feet fired. A blast shattered the air and the gun bucked. Zhiruto's chest blossomed into a hole.

"No!" Lora screamed, scrambling to her feet. This couldn't be happening.

But Zhiruto didn't let go of Randall's weapon hand. Instead, the hole shimmered, then closed up, just like in a scene from a Terminator movie. A stream of curse words left the agent's mouth, and he fired twice more —once to the head and again to the chest. Each blast opened a gaping hole. Each wound shimmered closed.

"Fuck me!" the guy yelled, and started backing toward her, firing at Zhiruto again and again.

Lora didn't have time to be shocked. Now was her chance. She sprinted out of the bushes and barreled into him. The gun went flying as he stumbled forward.

But instead of falling, he spun and struck the base of his palm into her collarbone. She heard a snap, and pain lanced down her arm. Gasping, she side stepped, barely dodging his next blow.

The agent bent his knees and brought his hands up, looking for a chance to strike.

She went into a half crouch, shuffling sideways to keep him in front of her. He'd obviously had martial arts training, and her kickboxing would be no match, but she had to try. She aimed an uppercut toward his jaw with her good arm.

He danced out of the way, aiming another jab toward her solar plexus.

Pain lancing through her from shoulder to hip, she lurched out of range in the nick of time. When the man darted forward again, she brought her knee up, aiming for his crotch.

He caught her behind the thigh with one hand, the other landing a blow to her cheek.

Her head rocked to the side and stars blasted across her vision, but she kept her balance as she yanked her leg free. Her broken collarbone was sending blinding white lightning into her chest and down her arm, and she could barely take a full breath.

From the corner of her eye, she caught sight of Zhiruto with Randall's head between his hands, bashing it back against the ground. But then she had to focus on her own opponent again as he bared his teeth and advanced. She widened her stance, staying on her toes. His hands were up, ready to strike. He was good.

By the look in his eyes, she realized he thought so, too. And it was just the weakness she needed. Guys like him were like cats; they loved to play with their prey.

Be the wounded bird. Not hard to do with the pain in her side and collarbone. Gritting her teeth, she forced her left arm up as if to throw a punch and whimpered, keeping her weight on the balls of her feet. When his attention shifted, she snapped her foot out in a switch-kick to his jaw.

The stars must've aligned just right, because her foot made solid contact. He rocked back, eyes glazing, then sank to his knees and toppled to his side on the forest floor. *Knockout.*

Except the pain in her side was now an agonizing knife in her gut. She doubled over, good arm clutching her middle. Looking down at her shirt, she realized it was soaked with blood, as was the arm she now pressed against the wound.

Her eyes refused to focus. She sank to her knees, panting as she tried to lift her shirt. But her fingers wouldn't cooperate. She looked up, trying to spot Zhiruto. The darkness felt like it was squeezing her, reducing her line of sight to pinpricks.

She slumped sideways onto a hip, barely able to support herself on her good hand. The ground felt so solid and good. She knew better than to sleep, but she needed to rest.

She'd only closed her eyes for a minute…

14

*L*ora opened her eyes to a pale purple ceiling. For a moment it felt as if she floated in thin air. Then she lifted her head slightly, taking in a narrow bed with soft raised bumpers on either side of her. The mattress was deliciously comfortable. She let her head fall back down. Where the hell was she? Her memories were a blur, but the last thing she recalled was kicking someone in the face…

Zhiruto moved into view above her, his dark eyes full of relief. He was shirtless, as usual, his broad shoulders and molded pecs as perfect as ever. "You're awake, Loragriffin."

The way he smushed up her name still made her heart flutter. She exhaled slowly. "Where am I?" Pepper's nose poked over the edge of the mattress, her urgent whine insisting on immediate attention. Lora scratched behind the dog's ears. "And how did you get here?"

"I retrieved her for you. We're on the IDA ship in the medical bay," Zhiruto said. "How do you feel?"

She had to admit, she felt pretty darn good considering she thought she might die last time she was awake. "I'm okay. Did you say we're on a spaceship?"

As if to prove just how weird her surroundings were, he pulled a floating stool over and sat down. "Yes. The healers extracted a bullet that had perforated your digestive system."

Remembering darkness and blood, her hand left Pepper's warm fur and reached for her own stomach. Her fingers met strange material, not quite silk and not quite velvet. She looked down and saw she'd been dressed in a soft cream-colored nightshirt. Sliding the hem up, she checked both sides of her abdomen; her skin was unblemished.

Then she realized her collarbone no longer ached, either. A broken collarbone would take weeks to heal. A gut shot even longer. *Thank God he remembered about Pepper.* "How long have we been here?"

"Two days."

Surprised it hadn't been longer, she sat up and looked around, fully taking in her surroundings. The walls were the same purple leaf-like texture she'd seen in the background on the video with Georgie. To her right, recessed shelves held an assortment of unidentifiable items. Another wall held a panel of blinking lights. She really was on an alien spaceship, and she really had been miraculously healed.

Then she remembered the way the bullets had gone through Zhiruto, creating holes that closed almost instantly. She turned her attention to him. "You took bullets, too. Are you okay?"

"I'm uninjured. Simple projectile weapons are ineffective against Kirenai. Our matrix can also absorb all but the most extreme blunt force trauma." He said it with pride, and she had to admit, it was sexy to have a boyfriend who was impervious to bullets.

Is that what he is? My boyfriend? Her thoughts felt both strange and right at the same time. "Thank you for remembering Pepper."

He smiled. "Of course. She's important."

She smiled back. He was thoughtful, protective, and sexy all at the same time. Squeezing her eyes closed, she fought back what had to be post-surgery brain fog. There were a whole lot of unanswered questions she needed answers to before she let these mushy feelings overcome her. "What happened to Agent Randall and his men?"

"His men are in stasis and awaiting justice. The emperor does not condone non-consensual servitude, and anyone caught participating in the black market trade will be punished." He looked away, his face grim. "Agent Randall is dead."

"You killed him?" she asked softly. She'd never killed someone in the line of duty or otherwise, but she'd met plenty of officers who had and knew there could be aftereffects.

"He was a vile representation of your species. I don't regret it."

She looked at him a heartbeat longer to be sure, then asked, "What about the assassin? Did you find him?"

Zhiruto shook his head, his lips forming a thin line. "Unfortunately not. Agent Randall put the creche holding the assassin on a separate shuttle, and no one seems to know where it went."

"Have you interrogated his men? We might at least be able to get a name."

Brushing his knuckles softly down her cheek, Zhiruto's eyes softened. "I was waiting for you to wake up."

She swallowed, feeling a bit stunned. Usually the men she worked with jumped at the chance to claim victory on an investigation.

She swung her legs over the edge of the bed. "We should talk to them right now. The trail's getting colder even as we speak."

"As you say."

She planted her bare feet on the strangely textured floor. "Where are my clothes?"

"I had some made for you." He guided her toward the blank wall and ran his fingers over some strange bumps. A panel opened up, revealing a narrow closet full of clothes. He pulled out a forest green tunic and matching slacks and handed them to her.

The fabric was as soft as the nightshirt she wore and stretchy like spandex, embroidered with a subtle wave pattern in silver along the seams. She eyed it dubiously, knowing it would cling to every curve, but it would at least be better than the long nightshirt she now wore. "Thanks. Where can I change?"

He pressed more bumps on the wall and a door slid open to reveal what looked like a motorhome lavatory. "My apologies for the poor accommodations. The IDA could offer no better options. Feel free to shower—I have not used our water allotment today."

She stepped inside and looked at the fixtures which were somewhat similar to Earth, but not entirely. "How do I turn on the water?"

He stepped into the small space behind her and reached around to point to some largish bumps on the purple wall. His nearness against her back made her skin heat with awareness; his blue, muscled arm was close enough that her own breath bounced back against her cheek.

Without even thinking, she leaned closer and kissed the inside of his elbow. "Thank you for saving me."

Two muscular arms wrapped around her from behind, pulling her back against him, and he nuzzled his face in her hair. "Thank you for not dying."

He felt so warm and solid, so alive, she couldn't help herself. She turned and put her arms around his neck, lifting her face to his.

Without hesitation, he claimed her mouth in a deep, satisfying kiss. His lips moved against hers and his tongue stroked forward with soft yet sure movements that soon had her panting with desire. He backed her slowly against the wall, one hand rising to cup her jaw while the other cradled her waist.

She let her head fall back against the hard surface as he pressed small kisses to the corner of her mouth and up her jaw. Her hands splayed over his back, loving the play of his corded muscles as he moved.

He nibbled her earlobe, sending a delightful shiver through her, then ran his hot tongue down her throat as the hand at her waist rose to find her breast. He cupped its heaviness before kneading gently until the nipple tightened in a hard peak. Rolling the bud between his fingers, he sucked at the base of her throat, his hard tongue massaging. She was probably going to have a hickey, but she didn't care. It felt amazing, like he was worshiping her.

She widened her stance, and he responded by leaning closer between her legs so she could feel the hard length of his arousal against her center. Her fingers clawed into his back as she flexed her hips, grinding herself against him.

He growled low in his throat, sending vibrations along her skin from his mouth. Dropping his hand from cradling her face, he hoisted her nightshirt up, pulling back only long enough to yank it easily over her head and off her arms. Then he claimed her mouth again, his kiss ferocious and intense as he plunged his tongue between her lips.

She realized she wore nothing underneath and now stood naked against him. His bare chest had a slight dusting of course hair that teased her nipples to excruciating awareness, and the heat between her legs was now an ache that needed to be filled.

Sliding her hands down to his waistband, she discovered he was somehow already naked. She didn't take time to worry about it and slid her thumbs along the slight indentation of muscle beside his hipbones to the top of his heavily muscled thighs. His hard shaft prodded against her belly, and she pressed it down until it tunneled between her legs.

He rocked his hips slightly, rubbing himself against her, and wetness flooded her pussy. His hands roamed her body, skimming delightful shivers over her skin as he slowly pushed his thickness deeper between her legs, sliding along her slit again and again until he was slick with her juices.

She was going to die if she didn't have him soon. Hitching a leg up around his hip, she reached for him, angling the head of his shaft into her opening. She gasped as he entered her, the fullness bringing her close to orgasm almost immediately.

Zhiruto hooked both hands under her ass and lifted her, settling her onto his cock as he stared into her eyes. Still inside her, he marched from the small bathroom back to the bed. He lowered her onto it, and the moment of broken contact made her whimper. "I want to taste you, Loragriffin."

Before she could reply, he placed his hands against her thighs and spread them, burying his face against her pussy. His tongue stroked up her slit and circled her clit before delving back down to plunder her with deep, penetrating strokes. Up and around he licked her, driving her crazy with desire until she was squirming on the mattress.

His lips wrapped around her clit and sucked while he dipped a finger inside her, the quick rhythm of his penetration pulling an unexpected orgasm out of her. She shuddered, legs going stiff as waves of pleasure raced through her.

Then he kissed her belly, pulling his finger out and climbing up her body until they were face to face. His stubble smelled like her, but she didn't mind as he kissed her, his hard muscles covering her with his strength and his cock settling between her legs. In a well-aimed stroke, he entered her, filled her completely, and she sucked in a breath of pure ecstasy.

He ground his hips, pulled back, and pounded in again, picking up a rhythm that had her crying out with every breath. The pressure inside her was rising to nearly unbearable heights as she lifted her hips to meet him, fingers digging into the tight muscles of his ass. She loved feeling it flex as he thrust, loved pulling him deeply inside her until there didn't seem to be enough air in the room.

Then her climax broke—the wave of her orgasm crashed down around her in a cascade of pure bliss. Her surroundings disappeared, and she knew nothing but him.

He drove hard into her, taking a few more strokes to find his own release, the hot jets of his seed filling her. When at last he collapsed on top of her, his heavy breathing a match to her own, she feathered her fingers down his flanks and kissed his shoulder.

He nuzzled her back. "My perfect mate."

The warm fuzzy feeling that gave her was almost enough to put her to sleep. Almost. "You told Agent Randall something about me having genetic markers. What did you mean?"

"I have implanted you with genetic markers that secure our mate bond."

A cold realization swept through her and she pushed against his chest to make him get off her. "Hold on. You implanted me something in me?"

"Yes, I told you after our initial intercourse." He lifted his head to look into her eyes. "You're the only one for me. I've claimed you as my mate."

There was that word again. Her heart fluttered and the familiar giddy feeling swept through her. But she wasn't going to let it take away her sense. Did he think he owned her now? She squirmed away from him and got to her feet, backing away toward the bathroom.

From where she lay near the door, Pepper raised her head, alert to the new tension in the room.

"I thought we already had this discussion. The auction wasn't selling slaves."

Zhiruto sat up, raising his palms as if to placate her. "Not my bondservant. My mate. Humans don't require permanent bonds in order to procreate, but it is the only way for most Kirenai."

She snatched up the discarded nightshirt and shrugged it over her head. "I'm not procreating with anyone."

"I'm explaining myself badly." He rose, his gorgeous blue body catching the light in all the right places. "We don't have to produce children. The genetic material we share will grant you longevity to match my own. We're bonded for life."

Her chest felt tight and her mouth dry. "Is that why I feel this way around you? Because you put some sort of DNA drug in me?"

His blue face had gone still. "Loragriffin—"

"It's Lora. Just plain Lora. And I'm serious. Get me off this damn spaceship, and take me home this instant. I want this disgusting genetic marker thing gone. Out of me. Now."

He stared at her a long moment before dropping his gaze. "You're right. I overstepped. I'll take you back to Earth immediately."

Right before her eyes, his nakedness disappeared, dark blue slacks and a shirt materializing over his body like magic. Without another word, he strode to the door, bent to briefly run a hand over Pepper's head, then was gone from the room.

And Lora wondered if she'd just made the biggest mistake of her life.

15

The maelstrom of Loragriffin's emotions against Zhiruto's Iki'i was indecipherable, but her body language was very clear. She felt angry. Betrayed. And rightfully so.

He'd formed a mate bond without her permission.

He deserved to be forever separated from the one person who could share his heart. She obviously didn't want to share hers with him. He wondered if it had something to do with the human capability to bear children without a mate bond. Such a bond meant nothing to them.

Unfortunately, his genetic markers were part of Loragriffin's DNA now and could never be removed. But she didn't need to know that. She didn't want to have children, so she'd likely never notice it was there. Because she obviously didn't love him.

She would be happiest back on Earth. He would report back to the prince. After that, who knew? He would hopefully be able to find a new job, a new purpose.

He ordered the ship's transport technicians to teleport Loragriffin—*no, just Lora*—and Pepper back to Earth. He didn't go to the transport chamber with her. He couldn't bear to face her, to see the distaste in her eyes when she looked at him. It was better to let her go without any more contact. *But I will always ache for her.*

A cup of Hypawan brew in hand, he paced the galley and waited for the techs to tell him she'd returned safely home. Once she was gone, he'd take a military shuttle back to Kirenai Prime. He still didn't know how he was going to break the news to the prince. He'd failed his mission, would have to resign his post, and had absolutely nothing to show for it. Kirenai almost never had a mate reject them, especially after the bond had been set. The shame of his situation was almost too much to bear.

Staring at the nondescript purple walls of the galley, he took another long swallow from his cup. The strong alcohol did little to dull his feelings, and for the first time, he understood why people sought out the smoky mindlessness of the many *ahen* dens on Sireta Prime. It would be so good to feel nothing right now…

"She's safely at the coordinates you provided, sir." An IDA tech spoke from the doorway, keeping a good distance between them. Zhiruto had barked at the techs earlier when they'd asked if he wished to transport with Lora.

"Thank you," Zhiruto attempted to infuse his Iki'i with gratitude. Much as he wanted someone to blame for everything that had gone wrong, the techs had been compliant with his requests, and the IDA medics had saved Lora's life. They deserved better than his ire.

He teleported over to a royal military shuttle for the long ride back to Kirenai Prime. The shuttle wasn't as fast as the prince's personal vessel, and he wasn't sure if he should be glad for the chance to think things over or worried he'd go crazy with the wait. As the ship was preparing to enter FTL, his personal comm alerted him that he had a call. He assumed it was from Prince Arazhi, but it was from the empress herself. Knowing this didn't bode well, he told the pilot to wait and answered.

The empress's alabaster face was lined by worry. "Zhiruto, there's been another assassination attempt on Arazhi."

Guilt flooded through him. He should've been there to protect his prince. "Is he all right?"

"He's in a regeneration pod, and the healers say he should recover. We've been told the attempt was actually aimed at the human he brought back, most likely to keep her from breeding. Not that that's an issue, since she's barren. Did you secure an alternate female as I ordered?"

Zhiruto grimaced. He hadn't liked the empress's order the first time, and he liked it even less now that he'd met the humans in person. "The auction was not for bondservants as we believed, empress. I was unable to convince a female to return with me."

She leaned closer to the camera. "You know what my son likes in a female. You must return to the planet and bring back a fertile human my son will accept."

His throat tightened as he remembered the condom during his interlude with Loragriffin. "Are you certain the one he chose is barren? Humans practice something called birth control."

The empress's lips curled with frustration. "Yes, we're certain. The healers tested her and said she's incompatible."

Zhiruto dropped his gaze. This was unexpected and terrible news. But he couldn't return to Earth. It would be too painful. "I will pursue the assassin, empress, but I can't return to Earth. I'm not welcome there." It wasn't the exact truth, but it was all he could offer.

"And I'm afraid I must resign from my post. I am no longer fit to be the prince's security officer."

"Why would you choose to resign now?" She scowled. "You've been a loyal officer for most of my son's life. He needs you now more than ever. Whatever happened on Earth can't be that bad."

He found he couldn't meet her gaze. "I have taken a mate."

There was a long pause. "And?"

His heartbeat thundered against his ribs. "She rejected me."

"*Kuzara*." The swear word coming from the empress's mouth was enough to make him look up. Her face was a mask of fury. "These humans are nothing but trouble. Fine. I'll send another emissary to secure a female. But you're still not allowed to resign. Arazhi needs you. Come back immediately." She ended the call.

Zhiruto lowered his arm. The empress might want him to stay at his post, but only the prince had the power to choose his guard. Once Arazhi learned of Zhiruto's many failures—especially his inability to change shape —the only logical choice was to let him go.

Heading to the shuttle's small galley to look for a drink, Zhiruto wondered if he might find any *ahen* on board.

ora felt like Dorothy in the *Wizard of Oz* as a gut-wrenching whirlwind seemed to yank her off her feet. One minute she was standing on the purple floor of an alien spaceship, and the next she was on her knees in the long grass of her front yard. She retched dryly, and Pepper shook as if trying to clear water from her floppy ears.

"Officer Griffin, are you all right?" Lora's neighbor called from her driveway.

The last thing Lora wanted right now was to deal with a nosy neighbor asking questions. Forcing a smile and waving cheerfully, Lora called, "Yeah, thanks."

Rising shakily, she hurried to her back door. The moment Pepper was inside, she closed the door and leaned against it, breathing hard as she stared blankly at her kitchen. Someone—most likely Zhiruto when he'd retrieved Pepper—had cleaned up the containers of fried chicken, but other than that, everything looked untouched. Her cell phone lay dead on the counter near the back door, so she plugged it in, staring at the screen as the battery charged.

Her mind kept rolling over and over the past few days. She should be more worried about what was going on here on Earth, but all she could think about was Zhiruto.

We're bonded. His words were branded in her mind. *You're perfect for me.*

He'd saved her life. Stopped a slave ring. And taken care of Pepper while she was unconscious. Fuck, he'd even been willing to let her lead the investigation, right down to putting on that silly disguise. And he'd respected her enough to let her go when she'd asked.

Bonded didn't mean bound.

Nausea welled up inside her. She looked at Pepper, who watched her from where she lay in the doorway between the kitchen and living room. "Think I made a mistake?"

Pepper whined softly, tail thumping the floor.

She glanced back at her phone, nausea intensifying as she realized she had no way to contact him. Did aliens even have phone numbers?

Powering on the phone, she waited for everything to load, hoping for a message. There were several, but none from Zhiruto. The precinct had left a voicemail checking on her—apparently Zhiruto had let them know she'd been injured and wouldn't be in for a while. Another thoughtful gesture that made her belly knot with regret. The last message was from Maise. "Lora, I really need to talk to you. There's weird stuff going on. Please let me know you're okay."

Lora grimaced, feeling terrible for putting her friend off so long. She hit auto-dial, but after several rings, the call went to voicemail. Figuring Maise might be up to her elbows in sudsy dog fur, she dialed the kennel.

Maise's assistant answered, "Yappy Hour Grooming and Dog Kennels."

"Hi, Ted. Is Maise around?"

"No. Haven't heard from her in a few days," said the young man as dogs barked in the background.

Lora scowled. "She lives right upstairs, Ted. Did you think to check on her?"

"Hey, what she does is her business. I babysit dogs, not people."

Frustrated, Lora hung up and grabbed her keys. Then she realized she was still wearing only a nightshirt, so she hurried upstairs and put on a uniform. If there was trouble ahead, she wanted to be prepared.

After loading Pepper into the back of her car, she drove to the small apartment above the kennel where Maise lived. When no one answered her knock, she glanced around before stretching to retrieve the spare key from the little birdhouse wind chime near the door.

Inside, nothing looked out of place. A used coffee cup sat in the sink. The dog bowl held some kibble that Pepper immediately gobbled up. And the unmade bed could've been slept in last night. "Dammit, Maise, where are you?"

Lora pulled out her cell phone and dialed again. The tune for *Bad Boys* started playing in the bedroom— Maise's personalized ringtone for Lora. Cold dread filled her.

"Shit." She spotted the phone plugged in on the bedside table.

Was it just coincidence Maise had gone missing right after the auction?

No. Lora knew in her heart that there had to be a connection. It could be anything from an alien kidnapping to Agent Randall selling her off before he died. For a fleeting moment, she wished Zhiruto were here to back her up. *Stop it. You don't need him.*

Pepper was pawing at some dirty laundry in the corner.

"Good idea, Pepper." Picking up some socks, Lora put them into a plastic bag, then hooked Pepper back to her leash. "We're going to find Maise."

They went outside, and Lora offered the open bag to Pepper to smell. "Go find her."

Pepper immediately put her nose to the ground and started down the stairs. Lora expected Pepper would head to the parking lot and the trail would go cold because Maise had been forced into a car, but the dog led her around the back of the kennels and down the sidewalk into a nearby neighborhood. Now that the aliens were officially gone, the city seemed to be returning to normal, although a few yards still held signs offering paid parking.

They walked at a quick pace, Pepper trotting along as if she knew exactly where to go. They crossed the bridge that led to the pulp mill. The air was breathable, but the sour stench grew more pronounced as the houses thinned to nothing and the weedy fields surrounding the plant took over.

"Are you sure this is Maise's trail, Pepper?" Lora shoved the socks under the dog's nose again.

Pepper bayed and pulled harder against the leash, tracking off the road toward a stand of young trees near the plant's fence. Someone else had been this way recently; there was a barely noticeable line of crushed stalks just off the trail.

Lora's heart thundered as she contemplated what she might find at the end of this path. The scene was feeling a lot like the true crime podcasts she listened to, and she felt for the gun at her waist, reassured by its weight.

They wended through the trees until they came upon a dry creek bed. Pepper easily trotted down the steep incline while Lora picked her way down more carefully. Then it was all she could do to keep up with the dog as Pepper bayed again and began running. Lora's feet pounded the earth, and she prayed over and over that Maise was all right.

They climbed out of the creek bed and went through more trees, finally emerging into a clearing in the middle of the woods. Pausing, Lora gaped at the perfect circle of crushed grass in the middle. In the center sat something that looked a little like a pale purple rosebud the size of a city bus.

Pepper bayed again and pulled against the leash.

Lora gulped. "Maise?"

Whatever she was looking at had to be alien. She imagined the rosebud opening and swallowing her friend whole, like something from *Little Shop of Horrors*. Was this thing a monster, an invasive plant, or something else entirely?

"Maise? Are you here?" She let Pepper pull her one step forward onto the crushed grass.

Without warning, the rosebud lifted off the ground. An invisible force rolled outward, shoving Lora off balance. She landed hard on her backside at the edge of the circle. Pepper yipped and cowered beside her. The rosebud hovered a moment, completely silent, then shot straight into the air and disappeared.

Lora realized her mouth was hanging open as she looked at the now empty clearing and sky. That thing had been a spaceship.

And she was certain Maise had been on it.

17

By the time Zhiruto reached Kirenai Prime, a lot had changed; the royal healer, Elthos, had been implicated in the assassinations, and Arazhi's mate, Georgie, was not barren after all. Now a royal wedding was in the making, and Zhiruto was torn between jealousy and happiness for his friend.

He strode toward the prince's chambers for his first meeting, taking in the familiar gray stone walls and purple doors of the palace. Kirenai in all shapes and sizes passed him in the hall, and he was once more surrounded by the flow of his people's Iki'i. It was good to be home, yet it also no longer felt complete. He was missing a vital piece of his future. He was missing Loragriffin. *No, Lora. Just Lora.*

His throat tightened. Now he was about to relinquish the last thing that meant anything to him; his position as the prince's personal guard.

He entered the prince's chambers to find Arazhi at his desk, several interfaces open above it. Dappled blue daylight played over the floor from the tall windows facing a veranda, and the sharp scent of *kuro* tea rose from a steaming pot nearby. The prince stood as Zhiruto entered the room, his blue-skinned human form dressed in what appeared to be gray slacks and a button-down shirt that matched the styles Zhiruto had seen on Earth. Arazhi and he had been close even before Zhiruto had accepted the position as his guard, and the familiar warm touch of the prince's Iki'i surrounded him like an embrace.

He returned the greeting along with a small bow. "My prince."

"I'm relieved you're back." Arazhi waved a hand at his desk. "This whole assassination conspiracy has been a nightmare, and I have no idea how to run the palace guard."

"I regret I wasn't there to properly protect you and your bride." Zhiruto cleared his throat preparing to voice his resignation, but Arazhi continued speaking.

"No need to be sorry. You were following another thread. Tell me what happened while you were on

Earth." The prince moved to the table with the tea and poured a cup for Zhiruto before sitting in a padded chair that had a view of the patio. "You said the assassin was a *burendo* last time we talked."

Zhiruto sighed and sat down opposite the prince. *May as well provide my report first, then resign.* He stared out toward the shady blue trees, trying to find his center. He'd never had to shield his Iki'i from his friend, but his roiling emotions were too raw to share. So he fortified his walls. "The report of a *burendo* was a clever misdirection designed to take me away from the center of activity." The memory of the supposedly poisoned Kirenai rising from the transportation creche just long enough to deliver the lie still stung. "I'm ashamed to admit it came from the assassin himself—I spoke directly to him without realizing it."

Leaving out the more intimate details about Lora, Zhiruto explained everything that had happened. When he got to the part about Agent Randall trading unwilling women, Arazhi sucked in an angry breath. "Reprehensible."

Zhiruto nodded. "Yes, he was an evil man. I'm not sure why I didn't sense his intent from the start."

Arazhi took a sip of his tea. "Might it have something to do with that pretty human you were with during our communications?"

Heat infused Zhiruto's face. "Did the empress speak to you?"

"My mother and I are not on the best of terms at the moment." Arazhi knit his brows. "Why?"

Now Zhiruto understood why Arazhi hadn't asked about Lora from the start. Picking up his teacup, Zhiruto stared down at the inky liquid. "You aren't the only one who found a mate on Earth."

"Aha!" Arazhi set his cup down with a thunk. "I wondered why you seemed to be so fixed in your human form."

Zhiruto's normal form at the palace was that of a Hypawa, his mother's species, with slender limbs and a mane of hair that grew all the way down his spine. The vertebrae between his shoulder blades itched with the memory. Strange and demoralizing to think he would never assume that familiar form again. He wondered what he was going to tell his mother.

The prince jarred him from his thoughts with a clap on the shoulder. "This is excellent news! Where is she? Georgie will be delighted to have a human friend."

The shield around Zhiruto's Iki'i slipped, spewing forth some of the guilt and shame threatening to consume him. "She did not wish to come with me."

Arazhi leaned back, but compassion flowed from him. "Well, humans are difficult. Georgie took a lot of convincing to accept me. Keep trying."

"I can't." His next words nearly wouldn't leave his constricted throat. "I claimed her without permission."

A spike of alarm flashed from the prince. "*Kuzara.*"

Zhiruto rose, keeping his eyes downcast. "She was very clear that she does not wish to see me again. I betrayed her by what I did, and I don't blame her for being angry. I also don't blame you for dismissing me from your service."

"Dismiss you?" Arazhi sliced a hand through the air like a blade. "Never. You are my most important, most trusted advisor. This has nothing to do with your ability to serve me."

"But I'm now trapped in this form." Zhiruto looked up, sure he'd see disgust in his prince's eyes.

Instead, he saw resolve. "I'm also human now, so it's a fitting form for you," said Arazhi. "You're to remain in my service. We will not speak of this again." The prince rose, moved back to his desk and pointed to a list of names on one of the interfaces. "These are the guards who were part of my security detail during the latest assassination attempt. Were you able to learn any names from the humans who were working with the assassin?"

Focusing back on work helped dull the ache in Zhiruto's chest. "No. But I've gone over the IDA's records and there's one person unaccounted for from the guest list—a Kirenai named Iroth. He's listed as a 'shipping expert' and I suspect he may run one of the smuggling rings transporting illicit slaves."

"How did a smuggler manage to get an invitation to the event? I thought the IDA required referrals."

"My guess is that someone tampered with the invitations. I need a warrant with your seal to dig deeper into the IDA's secure files."

"Done."

Just then a female voice spoke from the chamber doorway. "Arazhi, can I interrupt you for a minute?"

The human held a data pad in one hand and wore a pair of glasses that made her eyes look larger than usual. Her pale blonde hair hung loose around her face.

Arazhi broke into a smile, and a wash of love filled the room. "Georgie, come meet Zhiruto, my personal security officer."

"Good to meet you." She granted Zhiruto a tight smile before returning her attention to Arazhi and hurrying forward. "I've been inviting my friends to the wedding, and I can't reach Maise. Lora thinks Maise was abducted. Here, I want you to talk to her."

Loragriffin. Zhiruto felt as if the world were in slow motion.

Arazhi reached for the data pad. "This is Prince Arazhi."

Loragriffin's face appeared on the interface. From the angle of the data pad, she couldn't see anyone except Arazhi. "Hello, your highness. Thank you for speaking with me. I worked with your security officer here on Earth."

The prince shot Zhiruto a concerned glance. "Thank you for your assistance. What can I do to help you now?"

"My friend Maise was carried away in a spaceship. We need to find her before she's turned into a sex slave."

Zhiruto's stomach clenched. He'd been so concerned with escaping Earth, he hadn't considered that the slavers Agent Randall had been meeting were likely still on the planet.

Arazhi asked, "Why do you think she was abducted?"

"Pepper and I tracked her to a field by the pulp mill." Pepper's muzzle appeared briefly on the interface. "We found a spaceship. A weird purple thing that looked like a rosebud. It flew away before I could stop it. Can you track it down?"

The prince grimaced and shook his head. "Tracking a ship after it enters FTL is nearly impossible. We'll scour the shipping lanes, but I'm afraid you should prepare for the worst."

Georgie shook her head and stepped forward, a spike of anxiety slamming into Zhiruto. "No! We have to find her."

"There must be something you can do," Loragriffin added.

Zhiruto snatched the data pad from his prince's grip, turning it so he could look into Loragriffin's chocolate brown eyes. "This is my fault, Loragr—Lora." He caught himself before he said her full name. "I will find her, I swear to you. If it takes the rest of my life, I will find her."

18

*L*ora stepped off the spaceship onto the ramp, gaping at the spectacular blue forest all around the landing pad. The wedding was in a few days, and she'd come to Kirenai Prime to help Georgie with last minute details.

Three weeks had passed since she'd spoken to Zhiruto, and since then, his updates on the search for Maise came through Georgie. If Lora asked to speak to him directly, she was told he was otherwise occupied. *Classic blowoff.* But she couldn't blame him. She'd acted without thinking, without giving him time to properly explain. She was pretty sure she might've called him disgusting. If their roles were reversed, she'd probably give him the cold shoulder, as well.

But she couldn't get him out of her head. *Does he even still think of me?*

"Please proceed. I will bring your bags." A blue alien with long eyestalks and fingers like a gecko gestured down the ramp. The small crowd of Georgie's extended family was shuffling across the tarmac toward the huge stone palace like a flock of confused geese.

"Thank you," Lora replied in strange syllables that definitely weren't English; during the two-day trip here, she'd received a chip that allowed her to not only understand but also speak other languages.

She gripped Pepper's leash and moved forward. The dog stayed close to her side, ears pricked and nose sniffing a mile a minute. She'd been a bit dubious about bringing Pepper, but with Maise still missing, she didn't want to leave her fur baby at the kennel.

Variously shaped and colored aliens had gathered on the tarmac to either side of a path kept open by two orderly rows of guards. Many onlookers held parasols or wore large hats, and as the sun beat down on the top of her head, she understood why. She'd been warned the planet was hot, but now she wondered if her suitcase full of strappy tank tops and shorts had been the right choice—even SPF 100 wouldn't protect any exposed skin from this sun.

Ahead, the looming stone walls of the palace were covered in blue vines and magenta flowers. The massive purple doors looked like they were made of the same material as the spaceship she'd ridden to get here and opened to a courtyard shaded by tall blue trees. Gravel that looked like pearls created pathways through the moss growing around the bases of the trunks, and small yellow flowers sprouted with abandon across the grounds.

She'd barely taken two steps inside when Georgie broke from the swarm of her relatives and swept in for a hug. "Lora!"

"Georgie!" Lora squeezed her friend back, delighted to see her in person at last. "I can't believe I'm walking on an alien planet."

"I know right?" Pepper was having a conniption, whining and wiggling in her excitement. Georgie bent and rubbed her ears. "Hi, Pepper. How are you, girl?"

Georgie's dad came over, a gleam of sweat sheening his bald head. "Georgie, Aunt Bev has some questions about sleeping arrangements."

"Of course," Georgie said. "Let me show you the way."

Lora'd been cooped up on a ship with Georgie's family for two days, and though she didn't mind them in limited doses, she was ready for a breather. The shade here in the courtyard was nice, so she let the family go on without her. Pepper tugged her toward a small brook and lapped up a drink, then squatted and did her business on the moss.

Cringing, Lora glanced around to see if anyone had noticed. She didn't have any cleanup bags. But a stocky blue alien with massive sideburns seemed to appear out of nowhere and cleaned it up as if this sort of thing happened every day.

"Thank you," she said.

He bowed and moved on without a word.

She entered a small doorway into the palace where the others had disappeared. The minute she stepped inside, Pepper let out an excited whine and started pulling toward an open doorway to the left. The hall was a straight shot forward, and the noise the family was making would be easy enough to follow, so she let Pepper pull her over to see what was inside.

A familiar set of broad shoulders and long blue hair stood like a statue in the middle of what looked suspiciously like a small, unlit storage room. *Zhiruto.*

He wore a form-fitting white tunic and slim black pants with orange piping down the front crease.

Lora couldn't seem to inhale. Pepper's leash slipped from her numb fingers and the dog lunged forward, her entire body wriggling with joy.

Reaching down to rub the dog's head, Zhiruto didn't break his gaze from Lora's. "Lora."

His use of only her first name felt like a punch in the gut. She found herself saying, "You can call me Loragriffin if you prefer."

Something in his eyes shifted, a flash of emotion that was gone as soon as it had appeared. "I haven't yet located your friend. Please forgive me."

She shook her head and stepped forward, unsure how to respond. He was so stiff. So formal. The room was tiny, and his spicy, masculine scent permeated the air. "I believe you're trying. But I also know Prince Arazhi said it might be impossible."

"I won't stop until I find her." Taking a backward step, he edged around her and left the room.

Trembling, Lora remained still, trying to process what had just happened. Why had he been hiding in a storage room? The most logical explanation was that he was trying to avoid bumping into her. She rubbed the back of her neck. This was going to be a long and agonizing visit if he couldn't even manage to look at her.

Feeling shaky and uncertain, she hurried down the hall toward the chattering voices of Georgie's family.

The next week was a flurry of activity helping Georgie finalize things for the wedding. The few times Zhiruto was in the same room with them, he barely looked at her and always found an excuse to escape as soon as possible. Even Georgie noticed the tension, despite being wrapped up in her planning.

"What's going on between you and Zhiruto?" Georgie asked as she stood still for the dressmaker's final adjustments. Her bridal gown was gossamer thin, and millions of pearls had been affixed to the surface using some sort of alien technology to keep them from weighing the fabric down.

Lora shook her head. She hadn't told her friend anything because she didn't want her drama to ruin Georgie's big event. There would be time after the wedding. "I can't talk about it yet."

Georgie's pale eyebrows rose. "I can ask Arazhi to dismiss him until after the wedding."

"No!" Lora grabbed her friend's hand, receiving an annoyed glare from the dressmaker weaving a line of pearls along the hem. "Please don't say anything."

"Then tell me what's going on."

Lora looked away. "It's complicated. I promise I'll tell you later, okay? Let's just concentrate on you and the wedding."

Georgie let out a sigh. "All right. But if you change your mind, let me know."

Forcing a weak smile, Lora nodded. "Thank you."

That night was the rehearsal dinner, and after several run-throughs in the enormous amphitheater where the wedding was to be held, everyone headed to a small banquet hall in the palace. Georgie's Aunt Bev clucked over everything like a mother hen and had insisted on a formal seating arrangement. Which of course placed Lora smack dab next to Zhiruto at the dining table. Her heartbeat fluttered so erratically she thought she might pass out as she settled into the seat next to him.

He wore somewhat human-looking clothing, and the white button-down shirt hugged his biceps and shoulders as if they were tailor-made just for him. He'd pulled his long blue hair into a man bun, and the blue stubble along his jaw had been well-trimmed to frame his sensuous lips. Not that he turned her way to allow her a full assessment. He kept his gaze straight ahead, and the rigid set of his shoulders and corded lines of his neck very clearly conveyed his displeasure at her nearness.

She picked at the strange food on her plate, her appetite non-existent. Everyone laughed and chattered around them and their bubble of silence. The carbonated drink they were serving reminded her of champagne, but all she wanted was a beer. Which, of course, made her remember Zhiruto tilting back the bottle at her house. Made her long to go back in time and have a do-over.

Then an epiphany washed through her. She was stewing over what a man thought of her—just like her mother. The exact opposite of who she'd sworn to be. She shouldn't blame herself for his responses. She was the one who'd been wronged when he mate-bonded her without permission, and Zhiruto had no right to treat her like a pariah—to refuse to look at her or even speak to her.

For the first time all night she turned to look directly at him. "You could at least pretend to make small talk."

His throat moved in a swallow. Slowly, he pivoted to face her, all restrained muscle and broody eyes. "If you wish. What would you like to discuss?"

Her mouth went dry. *God dammit, why does he have to be so spectacularly handsome?* She clutched at the gossamer threads of her indignation. "Well, you might start by apologizing."

"For what?"

"For avoiding me. Everyone notices, and it's embarrassing."

His gaze roamed her face as if he was trying to memorize every curve and hollow. "I apologize. I find it difficult to be near you, but I will try harder if that is what you want."

She swallowed. He couldn't stand to be near her? Her heart felt like it was made of glass and was about to shatter. "Well, being around you is no walk in the park for me, either."

He leaned forward a fraction, still looking at her face. "I can't stop thinking about you."

A jolt of awareness raced through her. Her breath caught, and she had to force out a response. "In a good way or a bad way?"

"Both. I'm truly sorry I rushed our courtship." Beneath the table, his leg touched hers. Stayed there.

Oh, God, there was that giddy, fluttery feeling all over again. "I don't think you can call our time together a courtship."

His hand slipped from the tabletop and rested gently on her thigh. Heat from his palm seemed to radiate straight into her belly, and her nipples hardened. He licked his lips, and she couldn't help staring at the glide of his blue tongue over his sensuous mouth. "I would very much like your permission to try again."

The suddenness of this change frightened her and thrilled her at the same time. She glanced toward the others, who seemed oblivious to the sexual tension circulating between her and Zhiruto. They had a connection even she couldn't deny. A connection she craved. She met his gaze again from beneath her lashes and nodded. "Let's talk about it after the wedding."

His hand withdrew, leaving her bereft, but her heart swelled at the change in his demeanor. He smiled at her, actually smiled. "As you wish, Loragriffin."

19

Zhiruto didn't sleep a single minute between the rehearsal dinner and the wedding. Loragriffin was giving him a second chance. Whatever it took, however long she needed, he would find a way to be by her side. She made him want to be the best mate possible, and he would never stop seeking to please her.

He performed his duties for the prince, making sure everything was secure for the wedding. With over fifty-thousand citizens in attendance, he'd arranged many layers of protection to keep the royal couple safe. Now, standing beside his prince at the altar, he was impatient for the ceremony to be over so he could once more focus on his mate.

Loragriffin emerged ahead of the bride and glided down the aisle toward them. His cock hardened at the sight of her shapely legs appearing and disappearing through the long slit in the skirt of her magenta gown. Not even the bride in all her splendor could eclipse the stunning beauty of his mate, and he kept his gaze on Loragriffin during the entire ceremony.

She shot him shy glances throughout, and he could feel her yearning for him within his Iki'i. He'd kept himself closed off from her ever since their meeting in the supply room the day she'd arrived. Now he reveled in her attention. He would not waste another moment of their time together.

The wedding official pronounced the royal couple husband and wife, and Arazhi swept Georgie into a kiss that made the amphitheater thunder with applause from the audience. Then they turned and hurried toward the carriage Zhiruto had arranged to take the four of them away. Georgie had insisted on something called a "honeymoon," although apparently no honey or moon were required. He and Loragriffin would escort the royal couple to a secure location and remain nearby for the duration.

And he planned to use every scrap of free time wooing his mate back into his arms.

As thousands of glowing balloons fell from the amphitheater ceiling and the crowd continued its deafening roar of approval, he stepped toward Loragriffin and held out an arm.

She beamed at him with tears in her eyes. "That was so beautiful."

"Yes." He threaded her arm around his and led her down the path behind the prince and his mate.

He'd arranged for multiple carriages to act as decoys and ushered his mate into the one with the royal couple. As the carriage started forward and the royal couple were engrossed looking into each other's eyes, he turned to Loragriffin. "Are you ready to talk, Loragriffin?"

She smiled, affection warming his Iki'i. "Shut up and kiss me, Zhiruto."

Enraptured by the permission to touch her again, he slid his palm along her jaw to cup the back of her neck. Her skin was so soft, her hair like fine silken threads between his fingers. She was delicate yet strong. Resilient in ways he'd never imagined. That she was willing to even think about forgiving him for what he'd done was a miracle, and he would cherish her every glance, her every word.

But right now, she didn't want to speak. She leaned into him, chin upturned, and he brushed his lips over hers before claiming her mouth in a penetrating kiss.

*L*ora tossed the last bite of her *kazhitu* bun to Pepper and sipped the cool, fruity drink the funny alien named Deshel had given her. He reminded her of a house elf from *Harry Potter*, and she was tempted to give him a sock every time she saw him. But apparently slavery was an accepted thing on this side of the galaxy, and people willingly—even gladly—entered into contractual servitude.

Not Maise, though. Lora looked up at the brightening sky, feeling guilty for sitting here being waited on by servants while Maise was…

Lora didn't want to think about what Maise might be enduring.

"What are you thinking, Loragriffin?" Zhiruto set aside his data pad. They'd been working on open communication since getting back together; there had been too much misunderstanding between them already, even with his ability to sense her emotions.

"Worrying about Maise." She'd given up her job at the precinct to join a galactic task force focused on finding abducted women. Her team had managed to track down and rescue several human women, but none had been her friend.

He moved his chair closer and put an arm around her shoulders. He didn't say anything, just held her. They'd already been through his guilt and her worry a million times, and he knew all he could offer was a hug.

The cell phone in her pocket started playing *Jaws*, and she groaned. Her mom still insisted on using her cell number to reach her, and Zhiruto had arranged for calls to be routed through the interstellar communication relays to reach her. Although Lora would've have been just as happy to ignore it, Zhiruto insisted family was important, so she answered without looking. "Hey, mom."

"Lora?" Static made the breathless voice unrecognizable, but she could tell it wasn't her mother.

"Yes? Who is this?"

"It's Maise."

"Maise!" Lora pulled the phone from her ear to look at her friend's face on the display. "Where are you? Are you all right?"

Maise's raven hair hung loose around her face, and her eyes were red as if from crying. "Lora, we need your help."

Ahen - an opiate-like drug.

Ayabe - slightly astringent fermented leaves humans might think resembles cole slaw.

Bacca - a game that resembles frisbee golf.

Burendo - a Kirenai who excels at shapeshifting and is able to not only assume the form of other species, but coloration as well.

Fogarian - aliens with red hair and sideburns who live on a rocky, mountainous planet.

G'nax - a species that uses light to communicate attraction and arousal. They also have a symbiotic relationship with an eight-legged insectoid.

Hage - bald, wide-eyed alien that looks much like the iconic alien humans have circulated.

Happa trees - blue fronds resembling palms.

Hypawa - species with magma-colored eyes.

Ijin'en - four-legged herd animal raised for meat and well known for its stupidity.

Iki'i - empathic power.

Irn - a unit of measure. One planetary rotation around the Kirenai's sun.

Jiro - a unit of measurement equivalent to approximately two Earth hours.

K'ogai - the town near the palace on Kirenai Prime.

Kazhitu - nuts that look like sticky buns when baked. High in sugar, and tastes buttery and fruity.

Khargal - gray, horned aliens with stone-like skin and wings from the planet Duras ;)

Khensei - a toxin that causes Kirenai to denature into their resting state.

Kikajiru - my distracting one - a term of endearment.

Kirenai Prime - the Kirenai home planet. Purple and blue with swirling white clouds.

Klen - aliens who communicate via scent.

Kuro - a type of bitter, very black tea.

Kuzara - shit, damn, fuck.

Kryillian death swarm - tiny insectoid creatures that can kill a man within seconds by sucking his blood.

Matrix/cellular matrix - the term for a Kirenai's cellular mass.

Nilgawood - a tree used to make resin.

Oritsu - An expression of awe.

Popotan - the plant used to line ship interiors that provides oxygen, recycles water, is highly resistant to radiation, and can regenerate itself if damaged.

Qalqan - a species known for their healers. Good bedside manners due to their resistance to emotional fluctuation.

Resting state - a Kirenai's amorphous shape, like nakedness to humans, it is shown only to family or trusted friends.

Senburu - a galactic conglomeration of merchants who oppose the emperor's rule. Individual members are called *Senbur.*

Sireta Prime - a popular party planet.

Supo cloth - smart fabric for clothing that doesn't need buttons or zippers.

Teozhisa - a cart to carry people.

Tolonovone - a device that creates lighted markings on the skin. Used by G'naxians as part of their mating rituals.

Ukimi ice - beloved dessert with cool, spicy flavor like sweet mint.

Vatosangans - species with alabaster skin and blue or green hair who tend to be stocky or rounded. Planet is called Vatosang.

Zhinku weed - common in the popotan fields.

KIRENAI FACT SHEET

Kirenai are an all-male species of shapeshifters with a natural form (resting state) like an amoeba who usually assume a bipedal shape to interact with other species. Until the discovery of humans, Kirenai required a permanent pair-bond with a female of another species to produce offspring. All Kirenai traits are dominant and located on the Y chromosome; male offspring are fully Kirenai, while female offspring are fully of the mother's species.

Birth rates have been historically low, and over the ages, the population has been dwindling. Human females proved to be exceptionally receptive to impregnation, and do not require formation of a pair-bond to conceive. This has made Earth a target for black market slave traders who deal in "breeders." The Emperor has been making attempts to protect the population.

Regardless of the shape a Kirenai is in, he will be recognized as Kirenai by his skin and hair color. The most common hue is blue, although colors can be anywhere from mint green to lavender. Rare individuals called *burendo* can effect coloration outside this range. Kirenai blood is clear or slightly milky unless infected, when it grows murky to almost solid white.

All Kirenai have empathic abilities called Iki'i which make them capable of reading emotion and desire, as well as identifying individuals within their own species regardless of shape. This is the only Kirenai trait sometimes passed on to female progeny. The ability also makes the species as a whole consummate lovers because they can take actions and form attributes their partner finds most appealing. Bonded mates assume a permanent form pleasing to their mates; rarely can they force themselves into an alternate shape after bonding.

The average Kirenai life-span is approximately eight hundred human years. When a pair-bond is formed, a Kirenai passes a small genetic marker to his mate that mitigates the aging process, giving the mate a lifespan to match his own.

Dear Reader,

Thanks for reading Lora and Zhiruto's story. I'm working on book 3 in the series now - Iroth - which will publish at the end of October. If you want to read more from me right away, check out my other alien series, Galactic Pirate Brides.

With no females of his kind left, Captain Qaiyaan's fleet has turned to piracy and revenge. The last thing he expects to find on a derelict passenger ship is an alluring human woman carrying contraband technology. And he definitely never expected her to worm her way into his heart...

Tap the cover to get your copy now or keep reading for a sneak peek. (Psst - Book one is free right now!)

Until next time!
Love, Tamsin

"I recognize your ship, Captain Qaiyaan." The voice coming over the ship's comm deepened with menace. "You're interfering with a legal salvage operation."

The two ships rotating helplessly outside Qaiyaan's port screen told a different story than the human on the comm was telling; an eyeful of stars peeked through the blackened hole piercing the Syndicorp passenger ship's hull, while the second, unmarked vessel's short-range lasers glowed from recent use. "Seems you ought to be a bit more generous," Qaiyaan drawled. "What with needing our help and all. I'm gonna take first crack at the salvage, then we'll get you your part. You can have whatever we leave behind."

"I warn you, don't touch that ship!" blustered the voice on the other end.

Normally Qaiyaan'd wish the other pirate captain well and move on. Not today. His crew hadn't had a profitable job in half a Denaidan year. This opportunity was too good to pass up. Besides, anyone who blew a hole in an unarmed passenger transport—Syndicorp or otherwise—left a sour taste in Qaiyaan's mouth. "I could simply wait here. My first mate estimated in half a day we'll have two ships in need of salvage. This is an awful deep part of space to find yourselves without a spare flux modulator."

"You fucking son-of-a-rakwiji-whore bastard! I have powerful friends, and I can make sure you never find safe harbor in this sector again!"

Qaiyaan crossed his arms and glared at the comm. "I'm the *only* friend you have in the galaxy at this moment, so I suggest you be polite."

Noatak, Qaiyaan's first mate, grinned at him from the navigator's seat, the copper sheen of his skin reflecting the multi-colored light from the control panels. The small cockpit, designed for humans, was barely big enough for the two Denaidan males to breathe at the same time. "Want me to take us in for soft docking?"

Qaiyaan watched the human pirate ship complete another slow, helpless turn in the port monitor. "Take us in, but keep an eye out for anything suspicious. Could be a Syndicorp trap."

"Pretty elaborate for a setup." Noatak shook his head, the metal beads decorating his long hair and beard clicking softly.

"Chances of blowing both in-line flux modulators at once *and* not having a spare? Either he's stupid, or it's a setup."

"I say he's stupid." Noatak adjusted the controls to nose the *Hardship* toward the passenger wreckage.

Qaiyaan rose from the captain's chair. Shit happened, especially to ships running less-than-legal activities. He ought to know, having just forked out the proceeds from their latest heist to retrofit a new hull onto the *Hardship's* battle-damaged frame. The black market repairman'd all but asked Qaiyaan to bend over and spread his cheeks. Rotten, cheating bastard.

Turning to the door, he paused and looked over his shoulder at Noatak. "Just be careful. Even if it's not a trap, Syndicorp'll be looking for their missing ship, and I don't want to be caught with our dicks out."

After sealing the control room door, he slid down the ladder to the cargo bay, booted feet clanging against the catwalk grating as he landed. "Mekoryuk! Tovik! All hands on deck!"

Mekoryuk poked his clean-shaven face out of the med bay. He was the only crew member who chose not to wear the customary full beard the Denaida prided themselves on, citing a doctor's need for cleanliness or some such *anaq*. "What is it?"

"Salvage mission. Assume zero atmo. No time for suits. Syndicorp could be riding our ass any minute. Where's Tovik?"

"Where else?" Mek tilted his head toward the end of the hall.

Qaiyaan left the doctor and strode to where the hatch to the engine room stood open. As captain, he could appreciate the well-oiled hum of a ship's engines, but Tovik was a bit too much in love with moving parts. Squatting next to the hole, Qaiyaan yelled, "Tovik! On deck ready for void! And bring a spare in-line flux modulator! Now!"

Knowing his crewmen would comply without further prodding, he headed for the airlock. Through the portal, he watched Noatak guide the magnetic grappler into place. The captain of the human ship was probably apoplectic, watching his cash cow get raped by another ship. *Tough luck.* Qaiyaan'd be sure to leave the replacement flux modulator within reach, but not until the *Hardship* was ready to hightail it out of there.

The first mate finessed the grappler toward the other ship's open airlock, his voice crackling over the internal comm to the cargo bay. "You sure you don't want to take time to suit up?"

Mekoryuk arrived with a med-kit over his shoulder, and Qaiyaan shot him a grin as he answered. "No suits. These *qumli* need the practice."

Tovik pounded up, feet bare as usual, his scruffy beard and hair not quite the full mane of a mature Denaida male. Qaiyaan scowled at him, looking pointedly at his gleaming copper feet. The youngster said he had better control of his ionic abilities if his skin was bare, but one of these days he was going to lose a toe, or worse. At least the boy carried the spare flux modulator, as requested.

While Noatak secured the flexi-tube between the ships, Qaiyaan filled in the other crew members. "I'm not sure what we'll find over there, but it's not likely to be pretty. Grab everything not nailed down. We'll sort our inventories later."

Mek asked, "What about survivors?"

"There's no life signs aboard." Qaiyaan pointed to the modulator in Tovik's hands. "That'll stay with the human ship once we leave. Can you give it a slow push their direction? I don't want it to reach them until we're long gone."

"You bet, Captain!" the young man nodded, likely already calculating trajectory and speed at which to push the thing.

"Stand fast for void!" Noatak's voice echoed through the cargo bay.

Qaiyaan barely had time to summon his ionic shell before the doors cracked open. A blast of air swept past, rattling the flexi-tube as it sucked into the other ship and out the gaping hole in its hull. The Denaidan's ability to withstand vacuum had made them one of the most sought-after races for Syndicorp marine crews before the catastrophe had ended their world. Now…

Now they were just pirates.

Concentrating on keeping his feet on the deck, Qaiyaan tapped his temple to activate his cochlear implant. A vestige of his days as a trooper, it came in handy in zero atmo when they couldn't bother with suits and the attached comms.

The three crewmen pushed themselves along the flexi-tube into the darkness of the other ship. Tovik, ever prepared, pulled a floodlight from his belt and slapped it to the inner wall of the passenger ship. The illumination exposed a passenger cabin surprisingly gutted of anything passenger-related. No nav-grav seats for humanoids, no methane tanks for garan'uks, not even any acceleration webbing for yanipa-nimayu. Instead, cargo containers of all shapes and sizes floated freely within the cabin, some cracked open and spilling their contents in haloes around them.

What the hell is this ship? Qaiyaan wondered. He'd been expecting the gruesome sight of space-bloated passengers. Not that he minded this alternative. He reached out and grabbed a floating package of hypodermic needles. *Medical supplies?*

He exchanged a glance with Tovik, who shrugged. Whatever this stuff was didn't matter; he'd much rather deal with salable goods than corpses.

Qaiyaan pushed toward the nearest container until he could get a hand on it and shoved the man-sized box toward the flexi-tube, relying on inertia to carry it most of the way. One after another, he moved containers, working until sweat coated his skin beneath his ionic shielding. Even in zero-G, it took effort to hold himself steady and force the heavy boxes into motion. At least twenty minutes passed before he grew light-headed. Using the ionic shell was much like a diver holding his breath, and he knew they'd soon have to come up for air. A tinny voice in his implant did the job for him. "We have incoming on long-range, Captain. Can't yet tell if it's Syndicorp, but they'll be in range for ID in eight minutes."

Anaq. They'd come looking faster than he'd expected. He raised his arm and caught the other men's attention, circling two index fingers overhead to tell them to wrap it up. The men dropped what they were doing and moved toward the exit.

As soon as the door sealed, blessed oxygen began to fill the bay, but it would be a few minutes before there was enough pressure to breathe. Still light-headed, Qaiyaan began helping secure the containers against the floor's mag-locks. He estimated they'd emptied at least half the salvage and was feeling quite pleased as Noatak began accelerating away from the derelict ship.

"Captain?" Mek called from behind a stack of containers.

At that same moment, Noatak's voice crackled through the bay's comm. "Confirmed Syndicorp ship closing in fast. We need to burn, ASAP."

"We need five minutes," Qaiyaan said, assessing the remaining cargo.

"Captain!" Mekoryuk called again. "We have a problem."

"What?" Qaiyaan leaned around the corner. Tovik and the medic stood over a cargo box, staring down at a portal in its surface. Blinking red light bounced off both their faces.

Tovik rubbed his hand vigorously across the small window. "Is that a girl?"

"You've got to be fucking kidding me." Qaiyaan slapped a mag clamp against the container he was securing and stood. "A cryo-pod? Who the hell picked that up?"

"You said grab everything," Tovik said. He looked up to meet Qaiyaan's gaze. "Can we keep her?"

Noatak came over the com again. "Captain, they're hailing us."

Qaiyaan scowled and thrust a finger at the cryo-pod. "She's not a *netorpuk* puppy, Tovik. Just secure the damn thing so we can burn. We'll figure out what to do with it later."

"That's the problem," Mek said. "The cryo's failing. She won't survive a burn in this state."

"Fuuuck." Qaiyaan stomped over to the pod. He should have known things were going too easy. Looking at the face through the glass, his mouth grew suddenly dry. A young woman with long charcoal hair lay inside, a crescent of dark lashes against her high cheekbones. The blinking red light near her head illuminated her perfectly sculpted features as if coating them with blood.

"Just vent it," Noatak spoke over the line. "Let Syndicorp pick it up."

Tovik grabbed the end as if claiming the pod as his own. "You can't do that. What if they miss her?"

Noatak answered, "Not our problem."

"You should see what she looks like..." Tovik continued.

Now wasn't the time to argue over crew shares of the spoils, but Qaiyaan felt a sudden desire to wrestle the pod away from his engineer and claim the contents for himself. He tamped down the feeling. If they didn't get moving immediately, Syndicorp troopers would shoot first and ask questions later.

Noatak's voice boomed over his thoughts. "*Anaq*! They just obliterated the human ship!"

Syndicorp is out for blood today. Clenching his jaw, Qaiyaan shoved Tovik aside and began pushing the box toward the airlock, averting his gaze from the breathtaking face inside. "If we vent her, they'll have to stop and pick her up, which'll give us more time to get away."

"But, Captain—" Tovik started.

"We're not murderers!" Mek shouted, moving to intercept the box.

The comm filled the bay again. "Captain, you're not going to like this." Noatak's voice had gone from excited panic to deadly quiet. Qaiyaan ceased pushing, turning to face the speaker as if he could read his first mate's face from here. Noatak only used that voice when something deadly was going on. "They took out the passenger ship, too. There's nothing left of either vessel but a haze of space dust."

The breath left Qaiyaan's body. Syndicorp'd destroyed their own ship? Why would they do that?

Mek moved close to the captain, his voice low. "Venting her is a death sentence."

Qaiyaan squeezed his eyes shut. Why could nothing ever be easy? This woman was probably some scrawny human female on an exorbitant corporate cryo-vacation or some such nonsense. But he couldn't just leave her, not to the mercy of space, and definitely not to a ship that was blowing up everything in its path. "How long do you need to wake her?"

"The waking cycle takes twenty minutes."

He leveled a glare at the medic. "I didn't ask how long it takes. I asked how long you need."

Mek shook his head. "I can pull her out now, but she'll take days to recuperate. And she'll still be too weak to strap in for burn."

"Days to recuperate is better than minutes to end up as space dust. Pull her. We can link our ionic shells to protect her during burn."

Mek's right eye twitched. "We're exhausted from scavenging in zero atmo. I'm not sure we can withstand the strain."

"Do you have a better suggestion? If you do, make it now, because we're out of time."

"They'll be in range in thirty seconds, Captain," Noatak clipped out, his voice still deadly steady.

Mek's jaw bulged, but he nodded. "Fine. I think I've got enough stims to keep us up and running afterward. But let's not make a habit of it."

Popping the pod's seals, Qaiyaan knelt to lift the frigid human from the padded interior. She was naked, her nipples peaked from the cold. His hand slid beneath her nicely rounded bottom, every ionic sensor in his skin aware of the contact. He tried to remain focused on her face instead of the silky smooth curve of her hip cradled against his chest. Her eyes fluttered but didn't open.

Laying her on the deck, he stretched out beside her, grounding himself to the metal decking. Enveloping her in his power. Locking his body against hers.

Tovik sat cross-legged at her head, his bare feet tucked beneath him, and placed both his hands on her shoulders. But his gaze was on her upright nipples. Come to think of it, Qaiyaan's were, too, so he couldn't blame the young engineer. Mek spread out along her other side. An unfamiliar twinge made Qaiyaan want to shove them both away.

Hoping he hadn't just given all four of them a death sentence, Qaiyaan called out, "Engage full burn."

Get your free ebook copy from your favorite bookstore > Rescued by Qaiyaan

Galactic Pirate Brides series

Galactic Pirate Brides Box Set (Includes first 3 books)

Rescued by Qaiyaan

Ransomed by Kashatok

Claimed by Noatak

Taken by the Cyborg

Mates for Monsters

Mer-Lovers Collector's Edition (Includes first 3 books)

The Merman's Kiss

The Merman's Quest

A Mermaid's Heart

The Centaur's Bride

The Djinn's Desire

Khargals of Duras

Sticks and Stones

Alaska Alphas

Alpha Origins

Untamed Instinct

Bewitched Shifter

Midnight Heat

Wild Child

Kirenai Fated Mates (Intergalactic Dating Agency)

Arazhi

Zhiruto

Iroth

****POST-APOCALYPTIC SCIENCE FICTION WRITTEN
AS TAM LINSEY****

Botanicaust

The Reaping Room

Doomseeds

Amarantox

Once upon a time I thought I wanted to be a biomedical engineer, but experimenting on lab rats doesn't always lead to happy endings. Now I blend my nerdy infatuation of science with character-driven romance and guaranteed happily-ever-afters. My monsters always find their mates, with feisty heroines, tortured heroes, and all the steamy trouble they can handle. I promise my stories will never leave you hanging (although you may still crave more!)

When I'm not writing, I'll be in the garden or the kitchen, exploring Alaska with my husband, or preparing for the zombie apocalypse. I also love wine and hard apple cider, am mediocre at crochet, and have the cutest 12-pound bunny named Abigail.

Interested in more about me? Join my VIP Club and get free books, notices, and other cool stuff!

www.tamsinley.com

bookbub.com/authors/tamsin-ley

goodreads.com/TamsinLey

facebook.com/TamsinLey

amazon.com/author/tamsin

9 781950 027439